TODAY MY NAME IS BILLIE

TODAY MY NAME IS BILLIE

A NOVEL

Neile Parisi

GREEN PLACE BOOKS *Brattleboro, Vermont*

Printed in the United States

10 9 8 7 6 5 4 3 2 1

Today My Name is Billie is a work of fiction. Any similarity to actual
persons, living or dead, or actual events, is purely coincidental.

Green Writers Press is a Vermont-based publisher whose mission
is to spread a message of hope and renewal through the words and
images we publish. Throughout we will adhere to our commitment to
preserving and protecting the natural resources of the earth. To that
end, a percentage of our proceeds will be donated to environmental
activist groups and The Southern Poverty Law Foundation. Green
Writers Press gratefully acknowledges support from individual
donors, friends, and readers to help support the environment and
our publishing initiative. Green Place Books curates books that tell
literary and compelling stories with a focus on writing about place—
these books are more personal stories/memoir and biographies.

GREEN
PLACE
BOOKS

GReen
wriTers
press

Giving Voice to Writers & Artists Who Will Make the World a Better Place
Green Writers Press | Brattleboro, Vermont
www.greenwriterspress.com

ISBN: 978-1-7327434-9-6

COVER DESIGN BY ASHA HOSSAIN DESIGN LLC

PRINTED ON PAPER WITH PULP THAT COMES FROM FSC-CERTIFIED FORESTS, MANAGED FORESTS THAT GUARANTEE RESPONSIBLE
ENVIRONMENTAL, SOCIAL, AND ECONOMIC PRACTICES. ALL WOOD PRODUCT COMPONENTS USED IN BLACK & WHITE, STANDARD
COLOR, OR SELECT COLOR PAPERBACK BOOKS, UTILIZING EITHER CREAM OR WHITE BOOKBLOCK PAPER, THAT ARE MANUFACTURED
SUSTAINABLE FORESTRY INITIATIVE® (SFI®) CERTIFIED SOURCING.

*To my mother Nell—all that I am or hope to be I owe
to my angel mother, who has supported me and
been my greatest cheerleader throughout my life.
To my family, who loved and assisted me
continually. And to Elizabeth Taylor, who
always believed in me.*

TODAY MY NAME IS BILLIE

CHAPTER 1

Abuse at Home

I RAN AS FAST AS I COULD down the wet pavement, carrying only my purse in one hand and my toothbrush in the other. Still dressed in my nightgown, I had managed to don a coat, but there was no time for shoes. I prayed that Jimmy would appear soon as I fingered the revolver in my coat pocket. Breathlessly, I turned partially to see my husband chasing after me. *Oh, God, help me, please! Don't let him catch up with me. Jimmy, where are you? Hurry, please hurry!*

As I finished that silent prayer, a car rounded the corner, screeching on two wheels. The door flew open, and Jimmy yelled, "Billie, get in!"

The car kept moving and I jumped in, as if I were in a scene from a John Wayne movie.

"Hurry, Jimmy, he's gaining on us! I don't want to use this." I pulled out the gun and flashed it in front of Jimmy's face.

"Where did you get that?"

"I grabbed it as I was running out of the house."

I stared out the back window as my husband's image faded into the darkness, and for a moment, I felt safe. "He said he was going to kill either himself or me."

CHAPTER 2

William

IT FELT LIKE I HAD KNOWN WILLIAM my whole life. He and my brother were best friends in middle and high school. I never gave him the time of day; he was my brother's friend, not mine. I mean, I was polite, but that's all. He would come over to our house frequently. I didn't know why then. My mom always invited him for dinner. He liked being at our home more than his own. There was no drinking or fighting, only pleasant conversation and love surrounding our dining room table. We had a humble life, but we always felt the love of our parents. I think that was what William was searching for.

I was sixteen and he was seventeen, and like I said, I wasn't the slightest bit interested in him—but he was interested in me. He came over more frequently. This went on for two years. I had boyfriends and prom dates that didn't include him. When I graduated from high school, my mom invited him to my party. I went to a private girls' school. He went to the public school with my older brother. I started college in the fall, and so did William. He and I went to the same university. How convenient. It wasn't until sophomore year that I began to look at him differently, and he asked me out. I was nineteen and he was twenty.

He decided he wanted to join the army and was whisked away to Vietnam. He wanted to go. He liked being a soldier. He said it was the one thing he did very well. That both saddened and scared me.

He liked it so well that he signed up for a second tour. I wasn't sure I'd wait for him, but I did.

William was different when he returned home. He was nervous and defensive. I know he felt badly because people were protesting the returning vets. No one ever thanked them for their service. It must have been difficult being called baby killers. At times, he said he should have stayed there where he felt he belonged.

He was a highly decorated soldier, a green beret. He often said his greatest talent was killing, and his best occupation was being a soldier. That was why he did two tours in Vietnam.

William came from a tragic homelife. His dad, an alcoholic, died of cirrhosis. William was only thirteen when it happened. His mom drank and joined the ranks of severe alcoholism too. At this early age, he was raising his younger brothers and sisters, feeding them and escorting them to school, and filling in for both parents.

I attributed William's drinking to his homelife and tours of duty in Nam.

A couple of months after he got home, he returned to school, and we got engaged. The wedding was to be after William's graduation.

The abuse actually started while we were dating. The first time he hit me, he punched me so hard in the arm that it bruised immediately. I had to make up a lie to convince my mom that I had fallen and whacked my arm. That was a couple of months before the wedding, and my dad had a talk with him. He asked him if he loved me and wanted to marry me and take care of me. William apologized and said he did, so my dad gave his blessing.

I thought about calling it off, but foolishly, I didn't. I said to myself that the invitations had gone out, some presents had been received, and it was too late to cancel. We had an enormous and spectacular Italian wedding. It was so good, in fact, that the guests were reopening their cards and shoving more money into the envelopes. My dad owned a package store, so the liquor flowed freely. My brother paid the band to keep playing two hours longer, and the guests danced until the wee hours of the morning.

Everyone seemed to be having a grand time except me. William was drunk, and fell a couple of times on the dance floor. He spilled red wine on my wedding dress, and I cried.

When the wedding was over, I drove us to the hotel, where William promptly crashed and I spent my honeymoon night alone and sobbing.

It was an omen that he was so drunk throughout our honeymoon that we never consummated our marriage.

In this way, life continued for years of anything but marital bliss. The beatings began and continued.

William kept his gun under his pillow, and many a night, he'd wake up dreaming about Vietnam, yelling and screaming and ready to kill the Viet Cong. I was scared, and told myself I didn't think this could work. We would fight about it, and he would hit me again.

I knew his time in the service had caused much of the drinking. You can't have your best buddy blown apart in front of you and try to gather the pieces and feel normal, or see a child strapped to a bomb blown up as a booby trap. You can't kill day in and day out and expect to feel nothing. He was changed.

William trusted no one, not even me. He would drink during the day, and he would drink during the night. I don't know how he kept his job.

Holidays were the worst. We never quite made it to family functions, as William was usually drunk. I was so tired of making up excuses about his illnesses and problems. One Christmas Eve, I answered the phone to hear a police sergeant informing me that William had been arrested for drunk driving, and that I could pick him up in the morning at the station. So early Christmas morning, I grabbed his new down coat that I had wrapped for him, and drove to the police station to retrieve my husband. It was one of the saddest Christmases I can ever remember.

On another occasion, I had returned from our school bowling banquet to find him drunk and accusing me of having an affair with a fellow teacher, which of course was not true. We argued so intensely that the next-door neighbors screamed, "Shut up!" and "Go to sleep!" I hoped one of them would call the police to report the problem, but they never did, so I suffered in silence. That night was a bad one. He ripped my dress off, and actually pulled out some of my hair.

Time passed, things never really got any better, and after four years, I decided to file for divorce. I went home to my parents. William begged me to give him another chance, and said he'd stop drinking, so please come home. And I did. Two weeks later, he beat me so badly I had to tell my boss that I had been in a car accident to cover for the extensive bruises. I was so embarrassed that I didn't tell my parents; only my best friend, Lee.

My dad asked, "Do you love him? Because if you do, you need to try and make it work." So I tried. My parents liked him, and treated him very well. They didn't like the way he treated me. My brother approached him one day and said, "You have to stop—stop drinking and stop hitting my sister." My dad also told him to quit. He did, for a little while, and then he returned to his old ways.

Some of the worst beatings happened during the holidays. Those were sad days. I always felt so sorry for him, so I put up with a lot of crap, until one day I was praying, and the Lord said, "You were created to have joy and be happy on this Earth." That was the turning point. I said, "I can't go on like this anymore." It had been nearly five years that I had lived in fear and walked on eggshells.

I told William, "Either come to counseling, or I'm leaving."

He laughed.

I said, "I mean it."

So he sobered up long enough to come to counseling.

A good friend of mine had suggested that we try it. Of course, William accused me of having an affair with my friend. Any man I talked to was accused of being my lover. He thought the men in the bowling league, the bishop at church, and the other male science teachers were somehow all sleeping with me. I wouldn't have had time to do anything else if this had been true.

I wanted to try to make it work. I had been raised to believe that you don't get a divorce. You make your marriage work, especially if you have children. We didn't have children, because my husband said I would be a lousy mother.

I was so ingrained with this negative talk that my self-talk became negative, as well, and I believed him that I wasn't worth much. That no one would love me, and that I was lucky that he still wanted me. How powerful his words were.

I was so badgered that I agreed with him. He was right. I was of little worth. When the counselor suggested he come alone, he stopped coming completely.

Something changed, however. I prayed to feel worthy, and I received an answer. I was good. I had to leave. Another reason to leave him, but I stayed at least six months more, going to the counseling sessions on my own.

It wasn't long before William threatened to kill himself or me. He threw the vacuum cleaner through the living room window, broke some dishes and glasses, trashed the furniture, and grabbed his gun. I ran upstairs and called Lee's husband, Jimmy, to rescue me. Just then, William ripped the phone out of the wall.

He went into the basement, and I heard a shot. I was petrified, afraid that he had killed himself. I opened the basement door and saw him laughing maniacally. He was trying to punish me.

I ran upstairs. He followed me, grabbed a knife, and shoved it into his waistband, cutting his side. He had put the gun down on the kitchen counter. As he moved to the living room, I thought, this is my chance. I grabbed the gun and fled the house, leaving everything behind except my purse and toothbrush. I ran barefoot out the door, and this time, despite the advice of the counselor, I got a divorce!

So, I was very, very familiar with abuse and the nature of the beast. After this ordeal, I vowed I would never ever hit anyone or cause such sadness to another.

People asked incredulously, "Why didn't you fight back?"

"Why didn't you hit him?"

"Why did you stay with him?"

When there is addiction, you feel you can overcome it and change it, but you can't. You don't want to feel as if you have failed, so you stay. I did try to fight back. I tried very hard, but he was bigger and stronger—and when he was drunk, he was much stronger. So I would always lose, hoping it would change and be all better someday.

I learned some very important lessons from all of this. First, you can't marry someone and expect them to change, because they won't. No amount of love you give them can change who they are. Second, you can't believe the lies they tell you when they compare you to someone else. I learned I would always fail if I compared my weaknesses to someone else's strengths. Lastly, I learned that only I determine my worth. I gave my crown away, and let my husband crush it. He said things like, "You will make a terrible mother. I'd rather give my sperm to a whore than you, and fat women make terrible wives and mothers." I wasn't even fat, but I believed him. I fell into the trap. He said, "No one would ever marry you if you leave me." I believed him.

I left for good. I had the confidence to do this because I knew I was good, and deserved a better life. I didn't go back. I never regretted it. I wished I had left earlier. I thought counseling was crap, because the counselor had told me to return to our home and try again. I hadn't felt good about this, but I foolishly obeyed, and almost lost my life in the process. In the end, I left with very little, but I had my pride. And I changed my name because I knew who I was again.

CHAPTER 3

Philip

Philip was the sweetest, kindest, gentlest man I had ever known. He was such a contrast to William. Philip would never harm me, or even say anything hurtful to me.

I met him in school. We were both taking elective classes, unsure of a major yet. We sat next to each other in a general education class and started talking. The professor requested that we choose partners to work on a project. I spoke up right away and asked him to be my partner. He agreed. We met at the library three times a week to study, research, and prepare our project. It was great fun.

I started liking him, but was fearful, having been treated so poorly by William. But Philip seemed different: kind and gentle. We both hoped that we would decide where to concentrate our studies after these general education courses. One common characteristic we shared was our lack of self-esteem. We talked a lot after studying, sometimes in the library, sometimes at a coffee shop. We decided to be completely honest with each other and shared our tales, both good and bad.

We were both divorced, and had experienced feelings of great sadness. Each of us had been treated badly by our spouse. My husband had abused me, both physically and mentally. His wife had cheated on him and hurt him deeply, as well. It was good to discuss our pasts and to understand where we were coming from. Philip was seeking someone he could trust, who would adore him and not leave him. I was seeking the same thing. I wanted to be treated like a human being and be loved unconditionally.

Sometimes, the sunrise would end our talks. It didn't matter, because neither of us had anyone waiting for us at home. It felt good and right to be with Philip. We were both unsure of ourselves, but promised to support each other. We finished our project, scored an A, and decided we made a good team.

We chose our next set of classes together and finished the semester, still puzzled about our choice of concentration. I was learning toward law, and registered for some classes that I could use toward a law degree. Philip was leaning toward engineering. Between the two of us, we changed majors seven times. I thought I had made the right decision when I chose law, and Philip had been content as a math major. All of that changed, but we continued to see each other and help and support each other.

When school ended that year, we decided to meet each other's families. It was a pleasant experience for both of us. Unsure of what the future held, we continued to press forward, hoping we would guide each other in the correct way and stay on the path to success. We saw more and more of each other, and we found out that both of us had sought the help of counselors to free our minds and bodies, which had been damaged by our exes. We talked about moving in together, but that's all it was—just talk. Again, the feelings of inadequacy surfaced, paralyzing both of us. We would discuss it another day. Time was rapidly passing, and we were in our fourth year of college. Philip would graduate the following spring. I had two more years of school.

He finally asked me one day if I wanted children, and I nearly jumped out of my chair.

"Yes, oh, yes, I do! Do you?"

"Yes. I think we should get married. What do you think, Billie?"

"Are you proposing?"

"I think so."

"Then you must get down on one knee and ask me properly."

"Well, I don't have a ring."

"Well, you'll have to get one."

Philip knelt in the library on the cold stone floor and said, "Billie, will you type my term papers for the rest of my life?"

I laughed out loud, and agreed. "Yes, yes, I will!"

He stood up and hugged and kissed me. "Tomorrow, we'll go pick out a ring. I'm so excited. I can't wait to tell everyone."

I knew this would be a wonderful union, and we would be together for all eternity. It started out so perfectly. We had grown together and helped each other. Nothing could tear us apart, I thought.

I could see our unborn children in his eyes. He worked so hard as I attended law school and was so supportive when I decided I wanted to teach instead. A career in law was so all-encompassing, and there would have been no time for family. I hadn't learned to protect my calendar, and had already made myself readily available to my clients, letting my family come second. The grind of the corporate world didn't satisfy me as I had hoped it would. I needed more, so I explored another career. I decided to teach. Though the pay was so much less, the rewards were so much greater. At least that was my belief at the time.

Philip loved me. I knew it, and he knew it. He only wanted me to be happy. He never stopped applauding as he rose to his feet, watching me leap across the stage to receive my diploma. I had never felt more touched by his love than I did on that Saturday morning.

We had two wonderful sons who brought us such joy, and our marriage was strong. After all, Philip had been through some of the same things I had. I thought I could count on him, and that he would support me until the end.

Philip was an engineer, and worked with the phone company. He actually adored his job, and sometimes I called him a workaholic. Before I secured my teaching degree, he had been the one who was often late, calling to tell me he had to work overtime on a project. Now, the roles were reversed: I was often late. The fact that

Philip was such a good cook fit into the time slot nicely. He would start dinner, and got to spend time with our boys. They bonded quite successfully. In fact, it was an easy transition for them to spend their lives with their father.

CHAPTER 4

Teaching Eighth-Grade Science

TEACHING EIGHTH-GRADE SCIENCE was a joy. I was happiest when I was sharing my ideas with so many eager minds on a daily basis. Astronomy was my favorite unit to teach. Our annual field trip to the mountains to watch the stars, the phases of the moon, and possibly the alignment of the planets was well attended. Most students arrived early, with their permission slips properly signed in one hand and snacks in the other. Parents graciously chauffeured my students to and from the mountain location, despite the fact that the show began at 10:00 PM on a Friday night.

How blessed I was to teach these precious children, and to be in their presence. They had great faith in me, and believed that I had all the answers to the myriad questions they posed. This particular night was going to be exceptional, as we were expecting a special guest. The local planetarium had agreed to loan three of their high-powered telescopes, along with their top astronomer, for the evening. I was honored that he would actually be attending and answer all of my students' questions. While we waited for the conditions to be right and the equipment to be set up, the parents who had volunteered to chaperone were handing out steaming cups of hot chocolate and cider donuts. Some students said they came just for the treats.

What could have been better than this for any eighth grader—a Friday night under a crowded sky with friends and treats, and with me, magical, mystical Mrs. Murray, as my students had nicknamed me because of the experiments I performed in class?

Everyone was participating except Daniel Ray. This was the first time I noticed how sad he really was. He cracked jokes, hung out with the less admirable students, and was usually behind in his studies. It was as if he wanted to constantly be in trouble. He had come tonight without snacks, friends, or desire to learn. I guess it was a good excuse to get away from his homelife. He would do anything to be away from that environment.

"Hey, guys." He plopped down beside a couple of classmates. "This is so lame. What crap. You don't really expect to see anything in the sky, do you? It's a scam, just bull crap. I came for the food and to get out of the house."

"Why do you have to disrupt everything, Daniel?" one of them said. "Why can't you just enjoy it? You're such an ass. Why don't you just listen? Maybe you could actually learn something."

"Maybe I don't want to learn this crap. How is it going to help me, anyway?"

The astronomers had the three telescopes set up for viewing the heavens, and the students lined up, anxious to see the night sky. I was thrilled that these men had come on a Friday night to share their knowledge, equipment, and ideas with my students.

One student yelled, "I think I see Pluto!" The kids laughed as the astronomer explained that what he was viewing was a star. He continued to explain that the planets were stars, and that they had been researching what they thought was a new planet, as yet unnamed.

Everyone was eager except Daniel Ray. He meandered through the group, looking for his next victims to disturb. He had potential. He was so smart and promising. I knew I just had to convince him of it. I kept trying to engage him in activities that would help with his self-esteem and teach him that he was valuable. If I could only get him to abide by class rules, he could experience success. I just knew that I would reach him someday. He vied for my attention, but with a class of thirty-six students, he really didn't get that much. That was why I had designated him my class aide before and after school, and my timer in science class. I hoped that taking responsibility would heal him.

CHAPTER 5

A Typical Week

A TYPICAL WEEK OF TEACHING found me in my classroom every day at 6:30 A.M., preparing my experiments and readying my materials. Daniel Ray had asked if I needed help preparing, and I gratefully accepted his offer. This was my chance to guide him, assist him in building self-confidence. He was usually in trouble in his other classes; maybe this new job of teacher's assistant could change him. Keeping my fingers crossed, I proposed a schedule for him to work before school, after school, and during his free period. His parents agreed. Daniel's favorite task was to clean, label, and organize the test tubes neatly in their racks. His work was accurate, complete, and timely. As I said, he was bright and capable. I made sure he caught the last bus at 4:30, so he would be home in time for dinner with his family.

My day usually ended around 6:00 P.M., on a good day. Some days extended even later. I wanted my students to love coming to class. I was so proud of the fact that we usually won first or second place in the regional science fair, and the competition was always tough.

Philip was very supportive in the beginning, agreeing that dinner at 6:45 was acceptable; but after repeated late dinner entrances, he had demanded a change, and he was right. I tried to be home at 6:00. I really tried, and was successful for a while, but it was too easy to fall back into the old pattern. I just had to make a greater effort. I decided to go to school even earlier, knowing that it would put further strain on our relationship.

Philip sat me down and discussed this again. I was shirking my responsibilities as a mom and wife, he said. I needed to be more committed to my family than I was to my job. Of course, he was right, but how could I balance both? I certainly wanted my sons and husband to feel loved and important, but I also wanted my students to feel that same love. My boys had a wonderful father to fill in for me. Some of my students lived with a grandparent or aunt or uncle, and never knew the love of a dedicated parent. How could I fill everyone's expectations?

It's no wonder schoolteachers were required to be single in the old days; it was just too much of a commitment. I had an aunt who kept her marriage a secret for years so she wouldn't lose her teaching job. Imagine having to keep that a secret. What a lawsuit that would be today.

How could I have ignored Philip and the boys, been so unaware that we were drifting apart and that I was losing them all? I was so addicted to my work. It overtook my life.

CHAPTER 6

Experiment Lab

I LOVED EXPERIMENT FRIDAYS. These were the days
when I had experiment stations set up all around the
classroom, usually about eight of them. It took hours
to prepare, but it was so worth it to see the smiling
faces of my students as they understood a theory after
completing a physics workshop. I could see actual light
bulbs illuminate their eyes as they actively participated
in each experiment.

The students were organized into teams of six, and
a spokesperson was designated to announce their findings at the completion of the labs. Each week, there
was a new spokesperson. They would rotate around
the room through the various stations performing the
experiments, collecting data, revising their results, and
submitting their findings. Each experiment brought
them joy and amazement. That was how I had planned
it. I wanted them to experience the joy I had for science.

I wanted them to know that they could consider this subject with the knowledge that science can be fun and calming, yet exciting. I hoped that someone in the class would one day want to pursue a career in science and follow in my footsteps. The students were in awe of the results of their labor.

Everyone loved Experiment Fridays. Each student knew it was a time to support one another and share the joy of science. Everyone enjoyed this except Daniel Ray. He was the one who helped me set up the experiment tables early in the morning as my teacher's aide. He worked beside me to ensure that everything was perfectly correct; but on the day of the experiments, he was a tortured soul, begging for attention and wreaking havoc on everyone.

One such incident happened during a physics lab. The students were measuring the velocity of a cart filled with marbles as it raced down a course. Daniel was not very popular, and students didn't like him to be in their groups because his participation consisted mainly of fooling around. And so it was on that day.

"Hey, Mrs. Murray, Daniel is throwing marbles around the room. We are trying to measure the speed, and he keeps taking the marbles out of the carts. He's destroying our results! Couldn't you put him on someone else's team?"

"Let me talk to him. Daniel, what's wrong? You spent hours helping set up these experiments so it would all be perfect. Now you are sabotaging your team results. Why?"

"I don't give a crap about these experiments or about school. And I don't give a crap about you. And you don't care about me or what I do, so stop acting like you do. Nobody cares, nobody knows, nobody understands!" he yelled and ran out of the classroom. That was the beginning of his change—or had I not noticed the signs all along? He really didn't care, and he was going to make it miserable for everyone else. I turned to the class and announced to his lab partners, "Well, I guess you have one less teammate, so just carry on with your results."

CHAPTER 7

The Principal

MR. ANDERSON, THE PRINCIPAL, had an interesting effect on a person. If he liked you, you could do nothing wrong. He would praise you, show you off to others, promote you, reward you, and help you. But if he didn't like you, you would be ignored, punished, criticized, and removed swiftly from his presence and the school. I remember the day one of the other science teachers received a letter saying she would be transferred the following week to another school.

There had been no explanation. When she questioned it, she was told she was needed elsewhere. How could this happen? She had been at that school for nearly twelve years. She was set in her lessons and comfortable in her teaching. She had planned to finish her career there, and now she was being transferred not only to another school, but also to another grade level and subject. She was a seventh-grade science teacher. Now she would be a fifth-grade multi-subject teacher. What a travesty. She was a meek soul, and didn't resist. She just quietly packed her room and left. I was so sad to see her go.

CHAPTER 8

Daniel Ray

DANIEL RAY CAME FROM A BROKEN FAMILY. This may sound trite, but the truth is, I don't know how he even lasted to fourteen years old. He knew three fathers, and currently an "uncle" lived with them, his mom's latest beau. He had been in and out of juvenile court many times for shoplifting, possession, and neighborhood disturbances. His mom set a poor example for his brothers and sisters, and she found little time to encourage, help, or even love them. So Daniel found his own way to accrue attention, especially at school. He hung around with all the known troublemakers, defining his character by his crowd.

It came as no surprise when he was accused of stealing and cheating at school. He swore that he was innocent, and I was the only one who actually believed him. A suspension was ordered, and Daniel Ray became a distant memory at school. His crowd didn't care enough to talk to him, see him, or help him. His mom was aggravated that her son was at home, cramping her style. She screamed daily, "I can't wait for you to graduate and get out of the house." He admitted that he had once pondered suicide, but didn't have the nerve.

I felt such sadness for him, and in an effort to help him, I designated him captain of his science team. He himself hadn't even attempted to begin his science fair project, but he had tried to encourage his teammates, showing sincere interest in their projects. With little or no help at home, it was hopeless for Daniel to even consider a project. He had to spend his time feeding and taking care of his younger siblings. He was also the timer for his team. During the presentations, however, he was so distracting and noisy, it was as if he was begging to be thrown out of class.

"I'm not doing this stupid project."

"But you'll fail science class if you don't hand in anything."

"I don't give a damn. Who cares about science, anyway? You guys are wasting your time. I'd rather go out and get drunk." With that, Daniel grabbed a science fair board belonging to one of his teammates, ripped off some of the data, and threw it on the ground. A fight ensued, and punches were flying. I jumped in to try to break it up, and called the school guard to remove Daniel from the room.

I don't know what came over him. The guard had a difficult time escorting him out of the classroom. Later, I heard that he was uncontrollable all the way to the principal's office.

CHAPTER 9

The Fateful Day

THE NEXT DAY, FRIDAY, WAS A SNOW DAY—a welcome relief from the stress of preparing for the science fair, even though we would miss valuable time we could have had. On Monday, Daniel Ray was missing from class, but I thought I had seen him earlier in the day.

"All right, class, let's settle down and continue with the science fair presentations. I need a volunteer to be the timer. Okay, Tom, you can take over, thanks. Now, please try to stay within the five-minute time period. Steve, you're next: 'How the Salinity of the Salt Lake Affects the Brine Shrimp.'"

"Excuse me, Mrs. Murray," said Joann as she came in. Joann was a teacher's aide, and frequently helped out with classes. Her son was a member of the class. "Mr. Anderson wants to see you in his office."

"Now?" I asked. "We are in the middle of presentations, and the fair is in two weeks."

"He says it's important. I'll continue with your class."

"Thank you, Joann."

As I walked into Mr. Anderson's office, I felt a strange feeling of doom. I didn't know where this was coming from, but the feeling escalated to despair as I looked around the room and saw Daniel Ray, his mother, and his mother's boyfriend. Was I there as one of the people who would testify that he wasn't so bad, and that he shouldn't be suspended for fighting?

But that wasn't it at all. It was accusations against me. What was happening? What were they saying? Where was my union representative? My head was spinning, and it was all a blur. "I know who you are and how you treat your students. You flip out, holler at them, and touch them. You are a liar, and if I had my way, you would never be in a classroom again. My son has witnesses. Nobody hits my son, not even me!" (This was interesting, because a teacher had seen her slapping him during pick up time in front of the school after he got into trouble in another teacher's classroom.) She furthered her tirade by saying that she didn't know what my problem was, but I shouldn't be in a school. "You should be scared, 'cause I'll get you out of here. I'll have your job. You're going to get fired, and you deserve it, you child abuser."

Daniel chimed in, "Yeah, you're going to get fired. We're gonna sue you!"

What were they talking about?

There I sat, alone, no one at my side, no union rep, no fellow teachers, no Philip to support me—only the principal. Daniel Ray, his mom, and her new beau were all screaming at me. I should have walked out and demanded the presence of my union rep, but I was so overwhelmed by disbelief. I couldn't think, I couldn't focus, I couldn't even talk. I was in shock.

Finally, Mr. Anderson said, "Mrs. Murray, you are on paid suspension until further notice."

"What?" I said. "What are you talking about?"

"I'm sorry, we have to conduct an investigation because of the serious nature of the accusation."

"What accusation? What am I being accused of?" If they had mentioned it, I certainly hadn't heard it with the loud din running through my head.

"Daniel said you punched him."

"What are you talking about? I didn't punch him. Daniel, tell them this is a mistake. Please tell them this didn't happen."

"You're getting fired," he yelled and pointed at me. It seemed like this was the first time his mother had ever agreed with him, and he loved the idea. He chanted over and over, "You're gonna lose your job, ha ha, ha ha." It sounded demonic, as if he were possessed and couldn't control his speech or thoughts. He smiled and threw his head back as he continued to threaten me.

I felt helpless and crushed. I returned to my classroom, stunned by these words: *You are on administrative leave until further notice. You are not allowed in the school until the investigation is over.* The bell was pealing as I entered the classroom, ending the day and the week for me . . . and who knew what else it was ending.

Some of my students said goodbye. "See you tomorrow, Mrs. M."

"I guess we got out of homework tonight, ha ha."

"Stay cool, Mrs. Murray."

I don't remember answering any of them. I only remember the hole in the pit of my stomach growing deeper, and the disbelief rising in my throat and turning to nausea.

I sat at my desk, my head in my hands, and wept. I sobbed for what seemed like hours. I remembered hearing stories about teachers falsely accused whose careers were over even after they had been proven innocent. No one would ever hire them to work with children again. It was just too risky. You not only lose your job, you lose your career—and your life as you know it.

I had read about a daycare teacher who was accused of touching her students. She was promptly dismissed, as if she had never existed. She got off easy. She wasn't prosecuted, just dismissed.

Statistics say about 56 percent of the accused are innocent of the crimes, but 75 percent of accused educational workers either surrender their license or just get fired. Some say it's just too much trouble to fight, and chances are, no one will ever hire you again after you have been involved in any incident, even if you are not guilty. How shameful that all a student has to do is claim that he was mistreated, and the teacher is crucified for life. The student could dislike the teacher, he could be unprepared for class or just be trying to get attention, and the poor teacher is stripped of his or her career.

I read somewhere that tears can only flow for four to six minutes at a time. Mine seemed endless. My chest heaved uncontrollably as I screamed, "What am I going to do? Why is this happening to me? I can't believe this is happening. What am I going to do?" Over and over and over again, until I threw up. "How the hell did this happen? I hate him. He lied after all I did for him!"

I stopped crying and called my union president, who said she would call the principal, and, if necessary, send a letter to the assistant superintendent of schools.

Then I bowed my head and prayed, asking My Heavenly Father to help me through this ordeal, to know what to do and say, to confirm to me that I would have a job after the investigation was completed, that everything would be all right.

Then I heard a voice as clear as if someone were sitting beside me. The voice said, "YOU WILL LOSE YOUR JOB AND IT WILL BE VERY PAINFUL. PREPARE YOURSELF. PACK UP YOUR ROOM TONIGHT. YOU WILL NOT BE ALLOWED IN THE SCHOOL TOMORROW OR EVER AGAIN."

No, I thought, this can't be true, but a comforting voice assured me that it was to be. I actually realized that it was a blessing to know what was going to happen. I was prepared, at least for tonight. The next thing I was conscious of was calling my two best friends, Lee and Madge, to come by the school and help me pack up my room. I briefly explained what had happened, and they agreed to come by immediately. Then I called Philip, my husband, and told him I would be late. I didn't share what had happened. I wanted to do that in person.

CHAPTER 10

Packing My Room

LEE AND MADGE ARRIVED at around 7:00 P.M. with heavy hearts, open arms, and dinner in hand. We all hugged and cried for a while.

"So, what happened?" Lee asked. "No matter what, we will help you. We love you, and we will figure this all out."

"We're on your side, no matter what," Madge said.

"I knew you would be there for me. You always are."

We sat down and I told them my nightmare, expressing my anguish with the situation. I shared what I knew, and for the next four hours, my two best friends quietly packed up eighteen years of my life and my room, refusing to question me any further. They rejected the notion that I was guilty, and spoke of the future and my continued success as a fantastic science teacher.

As we rummaged through the boxes, I made decisions about what to keep and what to discard. There were experiments labeled for future classes. I loved being the magical, mystical mad scientist Mrs. Murray, threatening to amaze young minds with my experiments. I was a GRAND TEACHER. Students loved coming to my class. There were photos of science fair winners. We usually came in first or second. There were remnants of science projects, and much more. There were numerous textbooks—everything from the organs of the human body to the ten deadliest snakes in the world. There were rolls of adding-machine tapes that had been used to draw the phases of the moon.

Oh, how I loved astronomy. There were Styrofoam balls to make solar systems, every color of paint ever manufactured, and skeletal remains of various creatures that I had collected over the years. The biggest, and my favorite, was the skeleton of a wild boar with three of its four tusks still intact. I also had the femur bone of a horse, the horns and upper jaw of a steer that I had found in the desert in Utah, and complete skeletons of a squirrel, a bird, and a rat. They all had names.

And, I almost forgot—I had inherited a human skeleton, complete with skull. His name was Hector. There were booklets ready to use for compiling data from experiments. I always wanted to be ready. And let's not forget the glow-in-the dark paints, a smash hit used to create entire solar systems, a microwave and a bar refrigerator (necessities for any good science teacher), and more books on every subject: physics, earth science, astronomy, the human body, zoology, the earth, the sun, the stars, the moon, and on and on and on. Why did I need any of this anymore? Would I ever teach again? Should I just throw everything out and start fresh? I wanted to believe that I would be in a classroom again, but it seemed hopeless.

We continued to work in silence. I told our janitor Harry that I would be staying late, so he wouldn't worry when he saw my classroom lights on. Around 11:00 P.M., we wheeled my belongings and memories out to my car. It took three trips. Eighteen years of lesson plans, science equipment, rocks, plants, crystals, chemicals, test tubes, projects, weights, solar systems, demonstrations; numerous papers, books, and memories had all been reduced to eight boxes. We loaded them into the car, hugged again, and parted ways. I sat in my car for a long time and cried, and looked up at my classroom windows for a long time. They were dark now. And they would be dark to me forever.

I didn't get home until 11:15. Philip was waiting for me with a cup of tea and warmed-up dinner.

"Thank you, honey, but I'm not really hungry. I feel sick to my stomach."

"What happened?"

"It's such a nightmare. You know Daniel, my teacher's aide? He accused me of punching him. They told me I had to go home on administrative leave indefinitely until an investigation is complete."

I started sobbing, and Philip wrapped me in his arms.

"What? That's crazy. Tell me what happened. I just don't get it."

"On Thursday, there was a fight that Daniel started, and kids were screaming, swearing, and punching. I tried to break it up and restrain Daniel, and I had the guard take him to the principal's office. Then, today, I was called to her office, and there were Daniel, his mom, and her boyfriend. They were screaming at me and saying I was going to lose my job, and they were going to sue me. My head was spinning. I said, 'What are you talking about?' They told me to go home and not return until after the investigation. I said, 'What investigation?' I was helpless and hopeless, and went alone, with no union rep, no one to help me. I want back to my classroom, and the Lord told me to pack up my room, because they were not going to let me back in the school again. So I called Lee and Madge to come help, and that's where I've been all this time."

Philip held me as I wept. "Don't worry, honey. We'll call a lawyer in the morning. We'll figure this all out. It will be okay. Let's go to bed. It's late. I love you."

CHAPTER 11

The Lawyer

I CALLED A LAWYER THE NEXT DAY—the best in town, or so I thought. Attorney Barrone was known for defending teachers, and had a great success rate. He had been recommended to me. Several teachers had been reinstated as a result of his talent and legal skills.

I was mostly numb, scared, and disbelieving that first week. Part of me thought they would call me back and admit it had all been a mistake, and say I could return and take my rightful position in my classroom again. I missed my classes and teaching. But that was a dream. I was meeting the lawyer in two days.

I was still dumbfounded that Daniel Ray had accused me of anything. I thought he was doing so well. He had been my aide during his study periods, correcting papers and preparing equipment for experiments. He stayed after school to help, but had stopped coming early in the morning. He actually received two credits for being a teacher's aide. He had seemed more focused and to be enjoying school more and more. Why had he accused me of this horrific act? What had happened, and changed his feelings so drastically that he would lash out like this? Well, those answers would have to wait as I tried to defend myself and keep my job.

Philip sat, listened, cried with me, and cradled my head as I kept going over my saga. He also asked, "How did this happen? Why did this happen? What do you intend to do? Maybe you shouldn't have helped him so much. People start to think and wonder why you are spending so much time with him. What really happened?" It was painful to listen to Philip.

I never thought helping a student would turn into such a trial. I later found out that Daniel's mom's new beau beat him nightly. Daniel had said, "I hate the nights. I hate going home. I'd like to stay here as long as I can. It's happy here. I'm happy here." I didn't know then why he hated the nights. Poor, poor Daniel, to have to suffer so much.

I didn't schedule the bouts of depression, but with the regularity that they occurred, I could have sworn they were appointments in my daily plan book. I had read that the word depression is greatly overused and incorrectly used, but I had also read the symptoms of depression, and I was exhibiting every one of them, right down to suicidal tendencies. It seemed like a good plan to quietly slip off into dream world, never again to awaken to this nightmare. I just didn't have the balls to do it.

When my family was home, I learned just how loudly to turn up the radio volume, coupled with the shower running, so my screams were not audible to anyone. When I was alone, I yelled, cried, begged, and pleaded with the God I used to know and love. Why had this happened? How had it happened? When would I wake up? I couldn't survive this. It hurt too much. What could I do?

I washed, got dressed, and scoured the paper for job openings. I cried, read some more, and cried some more. I went to the bookstore and immersed myself in the latest bestsellers, hoping to find an answer, peace, solace, or just an excuse to stop crying. It was more difficult to cry in public, so I ventured out frequently.

CHAPTER 12

Philip, the Lawyer, and Me

PHILIP TOOK THE DAY OFF from work and accompanied me to the attorney's office. After listening to the lawyer, I realized that this was the first time Philip had doubts about what had happened. His eyes betrayed his words. He vowed his support. He mouthed the words I believe you, but his eyes spoke differently. They were hollow when he looked at me, and I knew he didn't believe me.

The attorney informed us that the Board of Education had an obligation to believe and protect the child, and my task was to prove my innocence. He also said it would be very difficult for me to win. I should have retained a different lawyer right then.

I only wanted to win my job back and salvage my reputation. That was all I cared about—not suing anyone. I felt that the principal should have defended me, but my attorney quickly educated me. His job was to defend the child. He couldn't have cared less about me and my future.

Now, the long, arduous task of defending myself began. At first, I had great faith in my attorney, but as the days progressed, I saw the pathetic truth. Everyone believed Daniel. No one believed me, except my dear friends and my mother. Would that be enough to maintain my sanity?

At this point, my relationship with Philip was crumbling. I was very hard to live with. I had no job. I read a lot. I cried a lot. I was in the way all the time. I kept crying. My husband suffered. My sons suffered. They didn't know me anymore. I couldn't play with them. I couldn't love my husband. I became consumed with the ordeal and the trial. I became the ordeal. I lost my identity. I lost my job. I lost my career. I lost my husband. I lost my sons. I almost lost my soul. That was all I had left.

My attorney asked a myriad of questions. "Did you punch Daniel?"

"What? I thought you were my attorney and believed me? No, I didn't!"

"I have to ask these questions. Why did you designate him as your classroom aide?"

"I felt sorry for him and his pathetic life. I wanted to help him. I thought I could make a difference in his life."

"Did you have feelings for him?"

"NO. Are you insane?"

"Just asking. Alright, tell me what happened that day in class."

I had gone over and over it so many times, both in my mind and with Philip, that now it felt like a memorized recitation. "We were holding science fair presentations, and Daniel was the timer. His job was to tell the students when their time was nearly up, and ring the bell when it was five minutes.

He started fooling around, taunting students, making fun of their science fair boards, and had actually ripped off some data when one of the students told Daniel he was going to fail because he had no science fair project. Tempers flared, screaming and swearing began, and then punches started flying. Daniel was pushing, shoving, and punching several students. I jumped up from my desk. By this time, there were eight students involved. I ran in between the students, holding them back, trying to restrain Daniel, and he was punched several times by the students. I yelled at him, reprimanding him for his behavior. At the same time, I called a student to go and get the guard. I told Daniel that he had to leave and go to the principal's office. He refused to leave. The guard had to physically drag him out of the room."

"Daniel told the principal that you punched him, and his friends corroborated the story," the attorney replied.

"I didn't, but he was punched several times by students. As the days progressed, Daniel was overheard by his English teacher coaching his friends in class as to what to say to the principal: 'Make sure you tell him that you saw Mrs. Murray punch me. I'll take care of you. Don't worry.' I later found out that the principal had interviewed these students, and they agreed with

Daniel. He also interviewed other students who sided with me, but apparently, their testimonies didn't matter. They told me I was on administrative leave until after the investigation. They feel they have to protect the child. Well, then, who is supposed to protect me?"

"That's my job. I must admit, it will be difficult, because he has witnesses who said you did it."

"But they aren't credible," I said. "They are his friends, and they would lie for him."

"Well, let's see how it goes in DCF Court. We will review the questions and answers with you a couple of days in advance. My retainer is $5,000 to start. You can see the clerk as you leave. I will call you in a couple of days."

"Thanks a lot," I said.

CHAPTER 13

Residual Effect

LEE HAD BEEN MY BEST FRIEND for as long as I could remember. We went to elementary school, middle school, and college together. We dreamed of becoming teachers one day. As young people, we used to role-play many times during the day, taking turns being the teacher or the student.

One summer, I even started my own summer school. I had fourteen neighborhood children. I charged them 25 cents a day, and I even gave them lunch! I certainly felt that this was the career for me.

At the time, it seemed that I was going to teach forever, and one day retire after many successful years. It was so satisfying. I would walk around the neighborhood picking up my students, their parents gladly escorting them out the door with their 25 cents held tightly in their sweaty palms. When we arrived at my house, we gathered around the picnic table so I could present the lessons for the day. The day always included something dramatic, with costumes and makeup. I usually let them write a short play, and at the end of the week, we would present it to anyone who would watch. This usually included my mom, my brother, and my cat. Even then, my cheerleader mom supported my endeavors. And she was paying for the peanut butter sandwiches and the lemonade.

Lee and I wanted to be teachers. It was a prestigious occupation then, unlike today's definition of the job. It was a time when children revered their teachers and parents respected them, again unlike today's standards. We were elated when we both graduated from the university. Now the best part was beginning. We planned to apply for jobs in the same school, and we actually were hired in the same school. I was an eighth-grade science teacher, and Lee was an English and history teacher. We were two of the finest teachers you could ever find: dedicated, intelligent, popular, creative, loving, and enduring. We were two of the most popular teachers in the entire district. I was even a runner-up for Teacher of the Year.

Lee couldn't believe it when I told her about Daniel. "They said what? Daniel accused you of punching him? What are they talking about? Everyone knows that Daniel is a liar, a thief, and a cheat. Don't they know that you are the grandest science teacher these walls have ever entertained? That is the best word to describe you—entertainer. Your students adore you and love coming to your class."

"That's true. They even come to school when they are sick so as not to miss my class. Remember when I dressed up as Einstein when I was teaching physics, and as Galileo when I was teaching astronomy?" I didn't have to wait till Halloween to dress up. It was a common occurrence in my classroom. I loved it, simply loved it, and so did my students.

I especially loved science fair season and prepping for the fair. It was our most intense time of the semester. Three-quarters of the students' grades were based upon their science fair project. Naturally, students spent a great deal of time preparing, creating, and researching their topics. I made myself available four nights a week after school to help my students.

Philip and our sons didn't see much of me during the science fair. He would make dinner for himself and the boys, and I'd grab something on the way home. He was very understanding, knowing how much this meant to me. I thanked him profusely when I finally arrived home. There were many late nights, and even more early mornings.

Lee said, "Billie, it shows how much you love science fair—you win almost every year. How could Daniel accuse you of anything? Wasn't he your aide?"

"Yes, I truly tried to help him, before and after school."

"You helped him too much. He was always in trouble with the law, his classmates, and in most of his classes. I remember catching him lying about a paper he copied. And Mrs. Burns said he stole money in her class. Well, I'm going to start a petition. I'll have the teachers sign it, and some students, to help keep you employed here. I'll write a letter of recommendation, and I'm sure other teachers and some parents will too. You'll see. It will work."

CHAPTER 14

Support from My Fellow Teachers

WHEN LEE ASKED MY FELLOW TEACHERS, whom I trusted, if they could write a letter, petition, or character reference for me, several graciously accepted. They arranged to meet me for lunch. They, too, were horrified about the accusation, and they didn't trust Daniel. He had so many issues with dishonesty, stealing, and cheating, and it was rumored now that he was involved with drugs.

Barbara, the social studies teacher, had overheard Daniel coaching his classmates to agree with him when he accused me of punching him. He had actually rehearsed what they should say to the principal.

"So when Mr. Anderson asks you to give your side of the story, just tell him how Mrs. Murray punched me. Got it? I'll make it worth your while."

"But I didn't see her punch you," David said.

"Just say you did."

"Okay, I will for you, Daniel."

My union president sent a letter to the assistant superintendent of schools after being told that the principal was not available to speak on the phone. In the letter, she listed all of the issues:

First, that the student went around the school telling the other students that Mrs. Murray was going to lose her job at noon.

Daniel Ray even boldly told other teachers that if they bothered him, they could end up like Mrs. Murray. He'd have them fired, also. He became more of a monster, thinking he was so powerful that he could control the teachers' futures. Of course, his mom fueled his behavior. He felt like he could do anything in any class and get away with it, and sometimes, he did. Some teachers were afraid of confrontation, and just ignored him. They were close to retirement age and frankly, just didn't want to deal with a possible issue. Take the Spanish teacher. Daniel got away with murder in her class, because she refused to give him any opportunity to hurt or betray her. She had one more year left until retirement, and she wasn't going to let anyone change that.

This was reported to the principal, and nothing was done to discipline the student. Apparently, he knew his parents were coming in to meet with Mr. Anderson, though Mrs. Murray did not know.

Second, no coverage was allowed for the union steward so she could attend the meeting. This is a violation of the Weingarten Rule.

Third, the woman who covered Mrs. Murray's class was a parent of one of the students in the class and a friend of Daniel Ray's. How many violations should I cite? What is happening here? This is intolerable, and the union is not going to take it. I want to know the names of the parents who supposedly called in complaining about Mrs. Murray, and with whom they spoke. I want all administrators to be instructed that they are not allowed to let a parent come into the school and berate and belittle a teacher. This is bullying and harassment—both very serious charges. I also want every administrator to be instructed on the Weingarten Rule, and to enforce it. I will be speaking to my grievance person and the union attorney as to what further action to take. I will end this by saying that teachers are being set up on a daily basis by kids who have their own agendas, fueled by the insipid means of doling out discipline. We need to change the climate in our buildings.

The letter sounded so powerful, yet nothing changed for me or my situation. Maybe future teachers would benefit from it, but I felt alone again, and let down.

One teacher in particular came to my defense. She was one of Daniel's teachers and had had trouble with him in her classroom. She insisted that she would not only write a letter, but that she would testify at the hearing for me.

She was told by the principal to mind her own business, or there would be consequences. This veteran teacher put her job on the line for me and lost her position at the school—the school from which she had planned to retire. She was transferred to another school for her kindness. How terrible that we had both now been eliminated from the school we loved. I felt so badly for both of us, but I couldn't help her. I couldn't even help myself.

Shortly after Lee testified on my behalf, she also was summarily transferred to another school. She was given the weak explanation that she was needed at another school. She was also told to mind her own business and let it go. Other teachers were also affected; the Italian teacher was told she was a terrible teacher. Rather than fight, she retired, even though she had planned to stay two more years. The third-grade teacher was told she was going to teach eighth-grade science, replacing me. She said she wasn't prepared, nor did she want to teach eighth grade, and left the school. The social studies teacher was transferred. The math teacher was harassed, hired a lawyer, and left temporarily on sick leave, but did return. Even the assistant principal was replaced. Mr. Anderson cited that he was also doing a terrible job so he left before he was fired.

Lee had taught there her entire teaching career, and had planned to retire from that school. Now, that was not going to happen. A total of five people were displaced, all because of the fact that they had come to my aid. What a weak, pathetic system we had. How could one principal be so powerful?

The Board of Education did not want confrontation, so they got rid of the trouble. I felt terrible that my friends had to suffer along with me. It was not only unfair, it was outrageous that one student could cause this much disruption. I was aghast that one principal could be so controlling.

My lawyer said it was similar to the Good Samaritan Act. The principal had to believe the student and protect the child. Even though Daniel had a reputation and a sordid past, I was already considered guilty. I had to prove my innocence.

The hell with me and my years of work and dedication. I didn't matter to anyone. I had lost everything, and no one seemed to care. It was over.

CHAPTER 15

DCF Court

I ARRIVED AT THE DEPARTMENT OF CHILDREN
and Families Court early to review the proceedings
with my attorney. He prompted me as to what I should
say. I wanted to give more details about the alleged
event. I wanted to tell the jury—three women and
two men—what had actually transpired that day, but
I was persuaded not to do so. Attorney Barrone said
it wouldn't help the situation. I knew the truth. "I was
there," I pleaded. Nothing happened. Why didn't they
believe me? I brought the petition signed by my fellow
teachers and the letter from Barbara, my fellow teacher,
along with me. Neither of these was permitted as evidence during the trial.

The petition stated that the faculty wanted to show
their support for me as a fellow colleague; that during
the past two and a half years, I had shown myself to be

a conscientious teacher who demonstrated great care for my students. I came prepared to share my scientific knowledge with my students, and the fact that, without hesitation, I was willing to help students study according to their individual learning styles. I had dedicated many hours, both before and after school, to making the lessons exciting and meaningful.

All of my lessons fostered student involvement. Those who knew me identified an individual in possession of a fine character. I had always exhibited ethical behavior, and cared deeply about every individual I taught. There were times too numerous to mention when I had tutored students for hours, allowing them to catch up with the class. In the classroom, I had adhered to the policies, procedures, and curriculum of the school district. I had a fine rapport with my peers, and worked cooperatively with them. For this reason, they had supported me in my endeavors. Many faculty members had signed the petition, and several parents had done the same. It was extremely supportive, but was still denied as evidence.

My attorney began with the statement, "The evidence in this case would permit a jury to find that the defendant had a personal agenda to injure the plaintiff; indeed, to remove her from teaching. He had been sent to the school by the superintendent with exactly that agenda—to "clean house" and remove teachers considered to be "troublesome" by the central administration. In fact, the plaintiff was only one of several—including the assistant principal—thus removed by the defendant in less than a year. Shortly before receiving that directive, the defendant had praised the plaintiff as a teacher. He knew that the student who alleged that the plaintiff had hit him was a notorious liar, who in fact had previously been arrested for making false reports at the school. He knew that another teacher had overheard this student coaching other students to lie and support his false accusations against the plaintiff, yet when that teacher reported these facts to him—prior to the DCF report—he instructed the teacher to 'mind her own damn business' and not to discuss this with anyone.

"The DCF report was immediately used by the school administration to remove the plaintiff from teaching and terminate her employment, without even awaiting the results of the DCF investigation. This pattern of behavior was seen by the Federation of Teachers as not only a violation of the union contract, but, in fact, a prohibited labor practice carried out to remove disfavored teachers in improper ways. The evidence in this case is more than sufficient to support a jury determination that the defendant acted maliciously and in bad faith in filing his DCF report. Accordingly, the matter must be left to a jury's determination, and the motion for summary judgment must be denied." I leaned over to my attorney and told him I had never even seen the report that was filed with DCF. He said he had seen it recently. Why hadn't I received a copy of it, so I could know what I was being accused of? He didn't answer me.

The first adjudicator began to question me. "So, you stated that Mr. Anderson observed your teaching in October of the 2003-2004 school year. Is that correct?"

"Yes, he came in October 2003. That was the only

time he came to observe me during the school year. But he never gave me any paperwork from the evaluation."

"Did you ever have any discussions with Mr. Anderson regarding that evaluation?"

"Yes. I asked him when he was going to give me the evaluation, so I could read it and sign it. He said he was behind in paperwork, and that he would get it to me shortly, but I never received it."

"Did you ever have any follow-up conversations with him regarding that evaluation?"

"He said I was a great teacher, and that Maria, who came to observe my class and my teaching (because I did not have tenure yet), also agreed that I was a great teacher."

Continuing on, he broached another topic. "So why did you persuade the student to be your aide?"

"I didn't persuade Daniel to be my aide. He asked if I needed help, and I did, and I thought it would help him to have the responsibility."

"For confidentiality purposes, we will just refer to the child as the student who accused you. I ask that that name be stricken from the record."

What bull crap, I thought to myself. His name is stricken from the record, and my name is repeated throughout the city, smeared and trampled upon? They are protecting his name?

"When did you first become aware of the DCF report that was made regarding your alleged hitting of the student in February of 2004?"

"When was I made aware of?"

"When did you first learn that a complaint had been filed against you with DCF?"

"The only thing that I was aware of was that the principal had said there was a complaint made about me. It wasn't until DCF called me for an interview that I was aware of a complaint filed with them."

"When did Mr. Anderson say there was a complaint?"

"The day after the alleged incident was a snow day, so it wasn't until Monday afternoon, when he sent a teacher's aide to my classroom to ask me to come to the office."

"Okay, and tell me what happened."

I had gone over this so often that I managed to tell it without emotion. I couldn't tell if I was believed or not.

"And what did Mr. Anderson do during this?"

"Nothing. He never tried to quell the anger, or reprimand the mother, or defend me. He did nothing except let her scream. Then the student chimed in, 'You're gonna get arrested.'"

"Why do you think he said you punched him?"

"Because he wanted to blame someone. He was embarrassed and upset, and I was an easy target."

"So you didn't punch him?"

"No. I didn't. I have a letter here from one of my colleagues stating that she overheard him coaxing students to lie to the principal."

"That's unnecessary," one of the DCF officials replied.

"How about this petition signed by teachers and some parents supporting me?"

"Again, this is not admissible."

"Well then what the hell is admissible?" I screamed.

"Back to the meeting with the parent, did the mother ever say anything about the nature of the complaint?"

"Yes. She said, 'My son said you punched him in the chest.' I said, 'No, I did not.'"

"Did you explain what had happened in the classroom?"

"Yes, I did."

"Were you angry with his behavior at this time?"

"I was upset that he was out of his seat, making noise, being disruptive, high-fiving students, swearing, ruining the science fair presentations, etc. I asked him to stop and sit down, and he wouldn't. Then he pushed another student, who punched him. Then others joined in, and all hell broke loose. I tried to break up the fight. I called the guard to remove him from the room."

"When you say guard, what kind of a guard are you referring to?"

"We have a security guard at the school."

"A police officer?"

"No, a security guard."

"Does he or she have a uniform?"

"Yes, he does."

"Did the security guard appear in your room?"

"Yes, and he pulled the student out of the classroom and took him to the principal's office."

"Were you present when Mr. Anderson interviewed the student or any of his witnesses?"

"No, I wasn't. I had no idea any of this was going on."

"I am handing you a document a copy of the complaint filed against you. Have you seen this before?"

"Not until just now."

"Do you have any information that leads you to believe that the report made by defendant, Mr. Anderson, to DCF was a false report?"

"Like I said, I never saw the report, so I don't know who made it and what it contains."

"Do you believe that the defendant knowingly filed a false report regarding this incident?"

"Yes. He did not investigate both sides; he only took the child's word and his friends. I think it was his explicit intent to get rid of me because of his personal agenda. Another teacher overheard the student coaching his friends as to what to say to Mr. Anderson. She wrote a letter to Mr. Anderson and gave it to him. The principal told her to mind her own business. That's an example of him not performing a complete investigation."

"Have you ever, as a teacher, received any training on when you are supposed to report acts of physical abuse or suspected neglect to DCF?"

"No, we haven't received any training."

"Do you know if you are a mandatory reporter under the Connecticut statute that requires certain individuals who have reason to suspect that there's been child abuse or neglect to report that to the DCF?"

"We don't report anything to DCF. We have been instructed to inform our principal if we suspect any form of abuse, and he takes it from there."

"Do you know whether or not the teacher's name who wrote the letter to the principal about the student's behavior in her class was ever given to the DCF investigator?"

"Yes, I gave it to him. But she was never interviewed. She even came to the hearing. When I tried to give a copy of her letter to him, his reply was, 'I know all about her. She is also bothering the student.' She was one of the first teachers to be reassigned to another school following the incident."

"Where was her classroom located?"

"Across the hall from me. She also taught eighth grade. She taught English."

"Was she in your classroom that day?"

"No."

"Would your testimony be the same if the matter had been reported to DCF prior to the time that the teacher contacted Mr. Anderson with the information?"

"Yes, but that is only part of it. Mr. Anderson knew about the student's behavior with coaching his friends, and ignored that information. But he also changed the wording on the evaluation sheets from the original ones. Let me explain. Remember I told you he observed me in October, and never gave me the paperwork to review and sign? Well, my union president asked for missing paperwork from my personnel file. She accompanied me to the Board of Education office, and we looked through my file. I had asked for the following documentation, which I never received: my evaluation, class management schedule, notes from a follow-up meeting with Mr. Anderson, and dates and observation notes from Maria's (who was assigned to observe my teaching) visits to my class.

"As we looked through my file, there was the observation sheet that Mr. Anderson had written talking about my excellent lesson, and what a great job I had done. I asked for copies of all of these, and was told that they would mail them to me. Both my union representative and I read the observation sheet. I should have demanded copies then, but they were insistent that they would copy the entire file and mail it to me—which they never did, even after repeated phone requests.

"Now today, the observation sheet you showed me is totally different. He changed the wording. This observation says that I was sarcastic with students, and that parents had problems with me. And that Mr. Anderson recommended that I have an aide and another teacher observe my teaching abilities. They said they were going to ask another faculty member to sit in on my classes, which is against union rules. None of this was in the original observation. He changed the wording to cover his behind."

"Were you on paid suspension when you had this meeting at the Board of Education?"

"Yes, it was a couple of weeks after I was suspended. And five in total faculty were reassigned or eliminated."

"Do you know if Mr. Anderson made reports to DCF against any of these other teachers?"

"No, I do not, but I think his behavior and conduct were extreme and outrageous."

"What do you think was extreme and outrageous?"

"He acted like he approved of my teaching. He came into my classroom, watched our experiment sessions, and said how great it was, that all the students were learning hands-on. Then, all of a sudden I was a terrible teacher, couldn't manage my class, had to be observed by other teachers, and was referred to DCF. He purposely ignored vital information, and thus caused me extreme grief and physical and emotional stress."

"Was there anything that prevented the DCF investigator from interviewing the other teacher?"

"I don't know. Like I said, she came to the hearing with her letter and the petition, and they never let her speak."

The judicator asked for a recess. My lawyer said, "Let's see what they offer you." Apparently, my fate was already sealed.

We were called back into the room after about fifteen minutes.

Judgment was swift and painful. In less than three hours, I was dismissed from my position and my career.

I lost my job, and it was very, very painful. I lost my income, my pension, my pride, my hope. I was left with one thing, though: a BIG BLACK X next to my name assuring me that I would never teach in this state again, and maybe nowhere else in the country.

My lawyer was useless and a disgrace.

"So, Mrs. Murray, we have decided that if you choose to resign and surrender your license, we will not fire you and you can withdraw your teacher retirement. If not, you will be fired, and another lawsuit may occur."

"What? What kind of deal is that? I lose my job and career, and I can withdraw my money and never collect teacher retirement. That is not acceptable. What about my reputation? I'll never get to teach again! I am known as a child abuser at this point. So my file says that? I have a record as an abuser?"

"It could have been worse. They could have prosecuted you and sentenced you to jail time," my lawyer quipped.

"Well, if they believe I'm guilty, why didn't they do that?"

"I don't know."

"I'll tell you why. Because some of the honest students told the truth. I never punched Daniel."

"I'm sorry. This is their decision."

"So my record says I punched him. Well, I'm not satisfied with this decision."

"You'll have to report to the Board of Education in a few days and sign the forms saying you choose to resign."

"But I didn't choose to resign; I was forced into it."

"I'm so sorry," my lawyer said, as he gathered up his papers and left.

Well, he got his $8,000, so he didn't care. I got nothing.

I wasn't done. I called my union president, and she called DCF and demanded that my name be withdrawn from the DCF Department's registry at the next administrative hearing. Several months later, I received a letter stating that the allegations were now listed as unsubstantiated, and that my name would not appear on a search of the perpetrator registry.

I went home after court ended and told Philip.

"Did they use the petition and letter?"

"No, neither. They said they weren't necessary."

"I knew you should have gotten another lawyer."

"He was the best in town," I replied.

Apparently, my fate with Philip was already sealed, as well. He was acting differently. It was obvious in our conversations and in our relationship. He acted embarrassed, and when people at his place of work asked questions, he didn't know how to answer them. He retreated from all activities in order to eliminate the conversations. He couldn't field the questions, so he stopped talking about any of it.

He asked, "So, what are you going to do now? Sit around and cry and read, as usual? Why don't you try to get another job—any job? We need the income. I don't know how much longer I can take this. Something has to change."

CHAPTER 16

Job Search

I APPEARED AT THE BOARD OF EDUCATION three days later and signed my career away. I surrendered my license.

I developed a routine for survival. Each morning, I would rise and pray for guidance. I didn't feel close to God, but I communicated regularly anyway. Then I would scour the papers searching for a teaching job. I did branch out in my search to include private and religious schools, but the pay was horrible and the duties overwhelming. One particular school was a charter school that required you to be there at 6:00 A.M. and stay till 6:00 P.M. for after-school activities. It was definitely asking too much. I decided to only apply to the jobs I really wanted to get, and not waste time on the others.

For three months, I applied to seventeen different school districts, to no avail. Each took my information, saying they would call me for an interview.

"Hi, my name is Billie Murray, and I am certified in grades one through eight. I have extensive training in eighth-grade science, and I'd like to apply for the open position in your middle school."

"Sure, have you filled out an application for the job?"

"Yes, I have, and I haven't heard from anyone in weeks. Could you please check for me?"

"Sure, hold on, please."

Thirteen minutes later, someone else returned to the phone. "I'm sorry to keep you waiting. We are reviewing your application, and will get back to you. Thank you." Click.

"Hi, I called last week about an eighth-grade science job, and was wondering if I can get an interview."

"Let me check. Please hold on."

Three minutes passed, and I heard, "Sorry that position has been filled." Click.

"Hello, I'm calling again about the middle school science job in your district—is it still available?"

"Yes. Let me have your phone number, and someone will call you for an interview."

None of them called. And when I called them back, they did not return my calls.

It must be true there is *still* a huge black X next to my name. The school board said that if I resigned, they wouldn't fire me. I had no choice. I resigned on the condition that the X be removed from my name. I had to surrender my license, never receive my teacher retirement, and stay off school property. All of these were conditions of the deal.

I made the choice to resign because I felt that being fired would be worse on my record, especially if I was ever going to try to teach again. The Department of Children and Families had agreed to remove the designation of child abuser from my records, but it made no difference. I still couldn't secure an interview with any Board of Education in the state.

It reminded me of the former mayor's son who was questioned in the case of the murder of his former girlfriend. Even after he was dismissed as a suspect, he lost his job, his wife left him, and then he ended his own life, professing his innocence till the end. How tragic.

How many innocent people have lost their lives to lies, false information, and pure evil? There is no restitution, only pain and misery.

In another case, two men spent twenty-seven years behind bars because they were accused of raping a young woman—they lost their case and were sent to prison, and then years later she confessed that someone else raped her and the verdict was overturned and they were released. But their lives were over, in a way: they missed births, birthdays, graduations, deaths, and moments in history they can never regain. One of them wasn't allowed to go his mother's funeral. The amazing thing about all of this is that the two men don't even hold a grudge. They forgave her and found peace in prison. They discovered God, religion, and solace. They were so young when they entered prison that it was the only home they knew. I hope they can write a book someday and be reimbursed for all the misery they endured.

For me, the greatest pain came at home. My husband and the boys didn't know me, didn't love me, didn't even like me. They didn't understand. During the day, I was either looking for a job or reading bestsellers. I thought, that's what I should do—write a book.

I lost track of time, and I didn't care. I spent most of my time away from home. It was too painful to see Philip and the boys. I knew I was losing them.

Philip wanted to talk one night. We hadn't really talked in a great while.

"Billie, this is very difficult for me. You know I love you, and the boys do, too. I have tried to come up with a solution to help us all. I have decided to take the boys to my mom and dad's for a while. We'll be leaving on Saturday. We need some time apart. I think you need some help. I can't help you. You need professional help."

"Please, don't!" I begged. "I'm trying to find work, really I am. Give me a little more time. Every day, I make progress. I think I'm going to write a book. It will help me to deal with everything that has happened."

"I've made up my mind. It's been six months, and nothing has changed. I don't know you anymore. You are so different. The boys ask, 'Where has Mom gone? What's wrong with Mom? Where is she all the time?' You don't play with them or talk to them. We just can't go on like this anymore. Please get some help. I'm sorry."

Philip held me in his arms for a long time and kissed me goodbye. I knew it was goodbye. I could feel it in his arms and see it in his eyes, those same eyes I had fallen in love with. His eyes, now crying, were incapable of lying.

Saturday came, and again I cried as I hugged my boys goodbye, assuring them that this would only be for a short while until I got a job.

"Take care of yourself, Philip. I'll see you soon."

I never got a job, and my family didn't come back. I knew I had to leave, secure a job, and start a new life, but where would I go? I was scared. What the hell was really going to happen to me? I threw a few things in my car and left. I didn't even look back, because I knew that my life there as I knew it was over.

CHAPTER 17

A New Life in South Carolina

I DROVE SOUTH FOR HOURS, and when I saw the sign for Easly, South Carolina, I had to stop. It was a quaint little Southern town where the kudzu climbed up anything vertical: telephone poles, clotheslines, even antennas. The people were warm and eager to help with directions, information, and local gossip. I pulled into the parking space directly in front of Mabel's Diner. A plump little waitress seated me, and immediately poured me a cup of coffee as the specials spilled from her mouth.

"So, tell me about the biscuits and gravy."

"They the best in Souf Calina," she announced proudly.

"Then that's what I'll have, thanks."

She quickly returned with silverware and a napkin.

"So what can you tell me about Easly, South Carolina?"

"What you wanna knows?"

"Well, my name is Billie, and I'm new in town. I'm actually looking for a job and a place to stay. What's your name?"

"Jessie."

"Pleased to meet ya. Let's talk about you, Jessie."

"Okay, Billie, but don't ya talk about ma cookin', ma body, or ma man. But y'all wanna talk about Jesus, I got lots to tell ya."

I laughed so hard out loud, and then I realized I hadn't laughed in over nine months. It sounded *so* good. "I'm going to like it here in Easly. So, where do you think I can sleep tonight?"

"Not at my place, Miss Billie."

Again, I laughed. Jessie recommended a motel where she worked her second job. The Thunderbird was neat and clean on the outskirts of town. She was right. She said if the train whistle didn't wake you, the hogs certainly would. Tomorrow, I would look for another home after I looked for a job.

CHAPTER 18

The Morning of My Birthday

THE MORNING WAS UNEVENTFUL. I continued with my usual routine. I was up early at 5:00 to unlock all the doors and turn on all the lights in the school. I had my coffee on the back stoop, watching the sunrise between the pines break through the pink sky, and thought about my family. Where were they now? Did they think about me, or was it so long ago that I was just a faded memory? I hoped my mom had kept my memory alive in their hearts. She tried to keep track of them, and sometimes told me of events in their lives.

It was the same for some of the students at Thomas E. Easly School. Several of the students were being raised by grandparents, aunts, and uncles. I wasn't sure if they even knew where their parents actually were. Some did know, but they also knew they didn't want to see them. Others begged to know who they were and where they came from. All of them felt some kind of love which helped them cope daily.

I also thought about Daniel Ray. What had happened to that poor boy? I no longer hated him. I only felt sorry for him. I learned to forgive him, the principal, and Philip. I had gained peace and power through forgiveness, but I was left with a massive hurt in my heart that never quite left. Poor Daniel. What a sad life and waste of a gifted mind. I hoped he had found help.

Where was Philip now? Where was his enduring love? It had been twelve years since I'd been with him. Six years ago, I managed to slip into a crowd and walk to the back of the bleachers just in time to see Max, our second son, receive his high school diploma. I wept as I cheered and clapped long after he had left the stage. That was the closest I'd been to him in twelve years. I missed him so much, and all the years of activities that I couldn't be a part of. It just wasn't fair. I told myself that someday, I would clear my name and regain my reputation. Today, I was wondering if that would ever happen.

Max was a genius in science, and I had often prayed that he would follow my footsteps and teach. Now, I wasn't so sure. To be honest, I wasn't sure about anything anymore. I was slowly losing faith that I would ever experience a normal existence again.

Joseph was our oldest son: bright, beautiful, and bodacious, as he described himself. He was a free spirit, and left home at eighteen to reform the world. The last time I saw him had also been twelve years earlier, when he was fourteen. I wondered what he looked like now, where he lived, and what he was doing with his life.

Luckily for me, his grandma, my mom, wrote to me often and called me weekly to keep me informed of the major events in their lives. She was the only one who believed me. Her voice was the most comforting sound in the whole world. When I spoke to her, I knew she loved me and that everything would be all right. I heard believable hope in her voice. She calmed the dark memories that clawed at my soul every day. She fortified me with her words. She said that someday, it would all be over, she just knew it. And I knew that when she hung up the phone, she wept, sometimes for days. Nothing compares to a mother's love.

Joseph wasn't at Max's graduation, so I assumed Philip had lost touch with him. Someday, I would see my boys again, and love them again. I wasn't so sure about Philip. I knew he had moved on, and rumor had it, he was now with someone else.

I myself had met a wonderful man, Jonathan, three years previously. He worked at the local grocery store—the only one in town. Jonathan was such a catch. He was a retired police officer who had lost his wife several years earlier. Because his children and grandchildren lived in South Carolina, he had decided to stay there. He had four children and ten grandchildren. "That's a lot of Christmas gifts!" he said with a chuckle. I thought, *I wish I had grandchildren. I wish I could still see my boys. Someday I would*, I promised myself.

He was a caring man who had lost his wife a few years back, and had always been lonely after that. We chatted as he bagged my groceries, and it took me over a year to finally say yes to his repeated offers of "coffee and."

I liked him. I wanted to let go of the past and be with him to be free of the darkness inside, but I had reason to be cautious, to abort any excitement, to protect myself from anything that might lead to another bitter disappointment. What if he rejected me when he learned of my past, even though I was innocent? I didn't feel strong inside.

We attended local school plays, which sometimes produced dark memories that possessed such power over me that I was reduced to tears. They rushed into my mind with such force that I became paralyzed and couldn't move. Would I ever be able to be around schools, activities, or even students again without experiencing a meltdown? Would I ever be able to teach again? Kind Jonathan waited patiently for me to stop crying. He never pried, just held my arm with a strong grip, comforting me until I was able to compose myself and stand.

Dear, sweet Jonathan. Someday, I would share with him the horror I had experienced, the fact that I had been swiftly discarded as a criminal, without a fair hearing.

We shared a lot though. We both loved plays and movies, camping and the outdoors, dancing, the shore, anything on the beach, craft shows, and good food. He was an excellent cook, and we enjoyed grilling all year long. The most important thing we shared was love for family. Could his family substitute for mine and satisfy my needs? I sure as hell was going to try to make it work.

Jonathan had a comfortable life. We had a great time together. He had a part-time job just to pass the time, and was always available to "come out and play" with me. We traveled a lot, visiting his family members. We'd go on weekend trips, often staying at Hilton Head and many other island spots. I loved my time with him, and often wondered if Philip was with someone now. He probably was, and that was good for everyone, I guess.

Jonathan was not the kind of guy I thought I would have been attracted to. He was a little shorter than me, and that had always bothered me in the past—but not now. He was also a little older than me, and that was a benefit. He had traveled all over the world and was happy to introduce me to new places, new food, new people. I remember the first opera he took me to. I loved it. He liked a variety of music, and shared it with me. I had always loved line dancing and country music. Jonathan surprised me on my birthday. He had taken dance lessons, and was now taking me line dancing. He was such an unselfish guy.

He knew so much, and so many people. I was fascinated that everywhere we went, he met someone he knew. He would casually say, "Well, you can't live this long and not know a lot of people. It comes with the age." I examined my life. I knew my family, some friends, and some teachers. I realized I had spent so much time talking to eighth graders, I had lost the ability to converse with adults—until I met Jonathan. He was now my hero, my guardian angel, my confidant, my friend, and my lover. I was so lucky—no, blessed—to share my life with him. Some of my happiest moments with him were spent just walking along the beach, holding hands and saying nothing.

Sometimes, I would ask about cases he had worked on. He asked why was I so interested in prisoners who were serving time for accusations of physical abuse. Someday, I knew I would tell him the whole story, but not today. I secretly feared that he would reject me if he knew the truth—but how could he? He was too kind for that type of behavior.

If I wanted this relationship to flourish, though, I would need to be perfectly honest. I didn't know if I was prepared for that. His family had welcomed me in all aspects of life. They had opened their homes as well as their arms, and invited me to all their family functions. They said their dad hadn't been this peaceful and happy since their mom had passed away, and they were indebted to me. The youngest children had started to call me Granny. It touched me so, and I cried openly.

I had actually started going back to church because of Jonathan's frequent invitations. He never gave up on me. He said I had to forgive God, because He loved me and had helped me through this journey.

I also had to forgive myself. I'd had my share of hardships and unpleasantries, but nothing this harsh or tragic had infiltrated my world until this experience. After that, I lost faith for a while. I knew I would someday return to church and God, but at that point, I had no interest in any God.

It wasn't so bad living in South Carolina. I had all I needed. I had my little home, and the lunch ladies always saved lunch for me. And boy, could they cook! Chicken-fried steak, biscuits, and gravy were my favorites. I painted my little cabin and built two large bookcases, which I filled with my favorite books—mostly science texts. I did so love teaching science.

When everyone left the school, I was free to roam

the library for hours uninterrupted. It was extremely pleasant, but I had to admit I was lonely for family and friends. I needed to change that, and change it soon.

I suspected that today would be like any other day, even though it was a special day. It was my sixtieth birthday. I whispered, "Happy Birthday, Billie," to myself as tears ran down my cheeks. Do you think anyone would remember my birthday? Do you think Philip and the boys remembered? Do you think they cared to remember? Did anyone here even know it was my birthday?

CHAPTER 19

Birthday Celebration

As I passed the kindergarten door, Becky Sue jumped out of the closet and yelled, "Happy Birthday, Miss Billie! I'm so excited to celebrate your special day."

She had made me a homemade card with the tiniest piece of lace taped to it. It was probably a treasure she had found and decided to give to me.

Soon, other voices joined in as I walked down the hall.

"Happy Birthday, Billie!"

"Thank YOU."

"Hi, Miss Billie, happy birthday!"

"Oh, thanks!"

"Hello, Mrs. Murray, have a great birthday!"

"Thanks for remembering."

I smiled, trying to feel cared about, loved, and important. But then, I was important—important to these children. After all, I had once been Billie, not just a janitor or teacher's aide. I had been a teacher, a friend, a grandma image. Twelve years earlier, I had been an eighth-grade teacher. And at that time,I wasn't just a good teacher . . . I was a great teacher. My students loved me, and I adored them. I spent countless hours after school explaining the phases of the moon, why dry ice was dry, or how a shark could sleep underwater. I loved teaching. I lived in my classroom, and I lived to teach.

And now, I could no longer practice my trade, my talent, my career. They had all been taken from me in an instant. It wasn't right, and it wasn't fair. How could this have happened? No one had promised that life would be fair and have a happy ending—only that we would have experiences and opportunities to grow and learn and teach.

I missed teaching. I missed molding and shaping minds, the minds of the children. I was heartbroken when I had to quit, so when I arrived in South Carolina, I naturally gravitated to a small schoolhouse on the edge of town. I walked in and asked if they needed a janitor or teacher's aide, a caretaker, or any position, because I needed them, and I needed a job. They didn't realize how much they needed me, too. Surprisingly they said they needed a janitor, and there was a little one-room cabin behind the school that I could call home. Oh, the tender mercies of God!

I had watched many children grow and graduate from that little schoolhouse. And today was my birthday, and the entire school was celebrating. Sweeping the halls, I looked around and noticed that all the students were wearing handmade badges that said "TODAY, MY NAME IS BILLIE." It touched my heart to know that someone cared about me and my birthday. I must thank Mrs. Baxter for spearheading this celebration.

The kindergarten students were the most excited, all wanting to show me their badges and asking me to call them Billie. They proudly displayed their badges, pointing to their names. I went along with the celebration, and I admit I loved every minute of it.

Then I heard an announcement over the loudspeaker: "Mrs. Murray, please report to the kindergarten room right away." I thought someone must need to be relieved, so I hurried to the room.

I burst through the door and heard the sweet refrain of "happy birthday to you, happy birthday to you." The entire school was there.

Tears welled up in my eyes, and I fielded questions between numerous hugs.

"How old are you, Miss Billie?"

"What are you doing for your birthday, Miss Billie?"

"Are you having cake?"

"Did you get any presents?"

I smiled at them all. "I'm sixty years old, and I'm having my party right now. I don't need any cake."

"Well, that is too bad, because Mrs. Baxter got you one. Just look at that!" squealed one little first grader.

Behind me, Mrs. Baxter and Mrs. Young were carrying in a huge birthday cake with several pink roses on it. It was inscribed Happy Birthday, Miss Billie. That's what they all called me there, and I loved it.

The children screamed with delight as I blew out the candles.

"You did it, Miss Billie!" yelled Becky Sue. "I knew y'all could. Make sure you save me a pink rose!"

Three students struggled to carry in an enormous birthday card, about three feet by four feet wide, complete with the signatures of the entire student body: sixty-one students, seven teachers, an assistant principal, and a principal. It was overwhelming.

I had longed for this attention, which confirmed that I was important, good, and deserving. No one here was judging me, suspecting me, or damning me. I was welcome, looked up to, trusted, and loved. I had forgotten what that felt like to be loved. I was so moved that I cried. I cried for my two sons, Max and Joseph, for my husband Philip, and for my lost career, which had spanned twenty-five years and included hundreds of students. I cried for all the missed holidays and events that had passed during the twelve years I had spent at the Thomas J. Easly School.

And yet I was extremely lucky to have a job; not a career, but a job, where I could influence so many eager minds craving knowledge. On any afternoon, you could find me with one of those eager minds, explaining or teaching a scientific concept or theory, and enjoying every minute of it.

"So, why are there phases of the moon, Miss Billie?"

"Well as the moon orbits the earth, its appearance changes, and we see a different phase each day. Maybe you could use this topic for your science fair project, since you are so interested in it."

"Yes, I'd like that. Can you help me?"

"Of course I can!"

The requests continued, buoying me up to the point where I actually thought I was still teaching! For a short moment, I allowed myself to feel joy, but it didn't last.

CHAPTER 20

Becky Sue

BECKY SUE WAS A DARLING, sweet girl with long, curly brown hair, big green eyes, and a smile that never ended. She had a space between her two front teeth that she called special. She said God made it just for her, so everyone knew it was her. She was such a happy child. She loved life and all it offered. She said "yes" to everything!

"Wanna act in our play, Becky Sue?"

"Sure, I do."

"Wanna play outside?"

"Of course."

"Wanna read to the other children?"

"Definitely."

She was smarter that most of the students in the school. She was different. She never complained, had positive words to guide others daily, and was always ready to help with whatever was going on at the time.

Her vocabulary was immense. She spoke as if she had lived many years on earth already.

I enjoyed conversing with her. She was entertaining and always had a tale to tell. She would recount stories, and you'd swear she had been a part of each one. She'd hear a story on the local news and retell it as if she were the reporter. Her rendition was so real. She could imitate anyone. Not just in the way she dressed, but in the way she walked, the way she talked, and especially her mannerisms. She proclaimed that one day, she would be a famous actress, and everyone believed her. I most definitely did.

Her grandmama lived with her, her four brothers, and her mom and dad. She said Becky was spoiled because she was the only girl. But who wouldn't want to spoil this precious child? At the age of five, she could tame anyone, teach anyone, and make anyone smile. Everyone wanted to either be with her or be her. I'd never met such a happy child. I wanted to be with her all the time.

She would run up to me in the hallway and throw her arms around my legs and squeal with delight every morning that she saw me.

"Hi, Miss Billie! How y'all doing today? I's just fine. Let me tell y'all what my cat did last night. She done ran away, but she returned with a friend. Can y'all believe her? Now, Mama says I have two mouths to feed and I'm in a mighty heap of trouble. Y'all want a cat?"

One day in the classroom, I heard Becky say to her teacher, "Miss Teacher, I ain't got near a pencil," meaning I don't have a pencil. She knew her kind teacher would have a pencil for her.

She came from a poor family. Easly was a poor town, but the children were happy. They had very little, but they had enough love to go around, and Becky felt that she was loved.

She was a special child. I looked forward to watching her grow and progressing into a fine young woman. I couldn't even imagine what she would become. She said she wasn't sure if she should be a princess, a doctor, or an actress. My bet was an actress. She could have been Scarlett in *Gone with the Wind*.

At recess, she was the one child who always invited the loner to join in and play games. There was one girl, Annamae, who had nothing on this earth. I don't think she even had running water in her home. Some of the kids would poke fun at her. They would say she smelled, but not Becky Sue. She would defend her, and say, "Come play with me. Don't you be crying now, they don't knows what they talking about." Soon, Annamae and Becky would be laughing and playing, and all was well. She had a way of making things all better. She was a special child.

"My daddy said they broke the mold when they made me," she would proudly proclaim. Her daddy was right. I wished I could clone her. What the world needs is many more Becky Sues.

I loved this child. If I'd had a daughter, I would have wished her to be just like Becky Sue. One day, she brought a present for me. She had carefully wrapped it in newspaper. It was a bracelet with some of the stones missing, but she had polished it up so it shone like the stars.

"I got this fer y'all, Miss Billie, 'cause I love you."

I put on that bracelet, and I never took it off from that day on. It made her so happy to see me wear it.

Every once in a while, you meet someone, and you know you knew them before this life. That's how it was with Becky. I know I knew her in the preexistence. I know we were friends there, maybe even sisters. We were kin.

I was so blessed to know her now. Even though I was fifty-five ears older than Becky Sue, there was very little difference in our ages. After all, she could have been in heaven longer than me and come to earth later than me. I could have sworn I had played with her at the Heavenly Father's feet.

I was so grateful and thankful to a Heavenly Father, who let me know I mattered.

CHAPTER 21

The Last Body

I GENTLY PLACED THE LAST frail body of a five-year-old on the wet, wrinkled, blue tarp. The fire department had provided it. Her body was as light as air. Being burned so badly, there wasn't much left to carry. The tears carved a path through the soot on my face and streamed down my neck. How could this have happened? How could we explain to Becky Sue's parents that their beautiful little girl would not be returning to their comforting arms ever again? How could this be real?

She was still wearing the badge in honor of my birthday. Though curled around the edges from the intense heat, the letters were still legible: "TODAY, MY NAME IS BILLIE." I had come to love this little girl. I imagined what she would look like at sweet sixteen. She was truly a Southern belle. I could see her at a debutante ball in all her finery, sashaying around the fine young men who wanted her hand, or perhaps just one dance with her. I could see her as a doting momma, loving and teaching her young-uns. She would have been perfect.

Now she was still—so still and quiet, yet so beautiful. Her long brown hair framed her face, which was covered in soot. Her green eyes were closed to the world. Her little body was half the size, but you knew it was Becky Sue. I was the last one to see her alive, and the first one to see her dead. I couldn't stop sobbing.

Now, this special soul was gone. I had carried her body out of the charred, smoldering shell of a building. Who would be there to welcome everyone, to help everyone? Who would smile at everyone and play with everyone? Who would compliment everyone, and tell us stories only the way she could? How would we go on without her? How could we explain what had happened, or why it had happened? How long would we have to wait until we saw her again? What would I say to make it better?

I was so terribly sad. I had lost a good friend. I knew I'd see her again, but I missed her too much. I wanted to rewind the tape and go back to the party, when we had all been happy. I wanted to hug her again, and hear her laugh and tell me stories. I wanted to play with her again. I wanted her back. The realization was that I wouldn't see her again on this earth.

I didn't hate God. I knew there was a reason. They say the Lord takes the very best souls early. They don't have to live a long time on Earth, because they have already perfected themselves. They just have to obtain a body, teach others, experience life, learn the lessons designed especially for them, and love others. Then they can return to Heaven, where they will welcome us someday in a glorious reunion in the sky. I knew this to be true without a shadow of a doubt, but it was still utterly devastating.

Many of the students had left early for holiday break the previous Thursday—a true blessing. No one knew where or how the fire had started, but it burned so intensely that we had little time to evacuate the building. I tried to save as many as I could, continually returning to the smoke-filled building over and over, over and over.

The volunteer fire department consisted of eight men. They rushed to the fire, but it was so intense, they had great difficulty getting through it. I wonder how many more lives could have been saved. What could we have done differently?

After a tedious investigation, it was believed that a birthday candle thrown in the trash in the janitor's closet could have caused the fire. It had smoldered in the trash, and filled the room with toxic fumes. Coupled with the rags and cleaning fluids, it had ignited rapidly, but gone unnoticed. My celebration had caused such a tragedy.

The kindergarten room was located at the far end of the building, the furthest from the exit door. Many of the kindergarten children did not make it out. I was able to help four of them from the building before the firemen arrived: two little girls named Dixie Taylor and Georgia Lawson, and two boys, Buddy Ray Preston and

Chase Jackson. Although they were soot-covered, crying, and scared, they were alive. They would return to their families that day. How lucky they and their parents were. I carried out three little ones who did not make it.

We lost eleven students that day, one teacher, and our principal.

CHAPTER 22

Aftermath

AFTER THE FIRE, life was different in Easly, South Carolina. We had not only lost Becky Sue and eleven other students, we had also lost Mrs. Augusta Blackmoore, a kindergarten teacher, and Mrs. Henrietta Calhoun, our beloved principal. School was canceled because of the tragedy, but it was also spring break, for which we already had five days off. It was not enough time to recoup anything. The devastation was beyond physical and financial; it was emotional and spiritual. The school needed extensive renovations, so we planned to move temporarily to a nearby building, the grange, to carry on classes. Other school districts provided some necessary items: books, paper, furniture, and writing utensils, but no frivolities.

It was difficult for our little town to hold so many funerals at once. Three of the families moved away, returning to their hometowns to bury their children.

Shortly after her funeral, Becky Sue's family moved away also. They say you can live all around the world, but when you die, you always go home, as indicated in the obituaries. We had eleven funerals to plan, attend, and deal with—a huge task for all of us to endure.

We only had one florist, one undertaker, and one cemetery, but we had seven different churches. The florist ran out of flowers, and had to ask other towns for help. The undertaker had to do the same. It took a toll on him. He said preparing young children for burial is always the hardest, and that he often cried through the entire procedure. He was glad to have the help of the neighboring towns. The assisting undertakers, three in all, graciously volunteered their services and talents. They tried to make the children look angelic, beautiful, and peaceful. It was the hardest task any of them would ever have to complete. I still don't know how they did it. They didn't sleep for a week, and when the families would show up with clothes, toys, and mementos for their children, they had all they could do to hold it together and not cry in front of the families.

Even with the donated services, there were still bills to pay. There were no Facebook or GoFundMe accounts to help—only good poor people who gave all they could to the cause. Between the *Easly Gazette* and word of mouth, most of the money was donated, and when there appeared to be a shortage, the Calhoun family (the family of Mrs. Henrietta Calhoun, our principal) humbly said they would take care of anything left. They knew the grief they were going through, and their mother had been quite old. They couldn't imagine what it would be like to bury a five-year-old. They wanted to help, and they knew Henrietta would have been happy with the decision. They even offered gravesites in their family plots for the children to be buried. Some of the parents chose to accept their gracious offering.

Of the seven churches, Easly United Methodist, Abundant Life Baptist, All Souls Pentecostal, Pendleton Street Presbyterian, The Lutheran Bible Church, Seventh-Day Adventist, and and All Saints Episcopal Church—all but the Seventh-Day and the Pentecostal churches—held the funerals. I was always fascinated that there were so many religions and a church on every corner here in this little town of Easly. Why couldn't they all believe in the same God? Why couldn't they all worship together? But now, it was a blessing to have so many pastors and churches to handle the funerals and the grief. The preachers spread out the funerals so we could attend several in one day. There just wasn't any way to cope with this except forgiveness. That was the recurring theme in most of the sermons. We had to forgive God, ourselves, and everyone involved. There was no other way to achieve peace and survive without forgiveness.

Mrs. Henrietta Calhoun had been a fine Southern lady. Her reputation was known throughout the South, not just in South Carolina. She claimed she could trace her genealogy from Adam to present times, and actually claimed that the Garden of Eden was in South Carolina, not far from where she was raised. She came from a well-to-do Southern family, prim and proper.

There had been many photos on her office desk, and a number of them were displayed at her funeral. They depicted the events in her life. Some of her favorites had been of her debutante ball, or cotillion, as they referred to it in the South. She actually married her escort, Samuel Calhoun. They were sweethearts, and were together sixty years and raised seven young ones who all went on to live memorable lives and made the Calhouns very proud. They produced twenty-five grandchildren and five great-grandchildren . . . her joy. Nothing was more important than family.

Then there was the last family portrait taken before Mr. Calhoun passed. There was an enormous live oak tree on their estate, with clumps of Spanish moss hanging from nearly all the branches. The grandchildren and great-grandchildren who were old enough were seated in the branches, and their parents and grandparents sat in front of the "Family Tree," as they called it. Everyone in the family was in attendance. The Calhoun family had the largest pecan plantation in South Carolina and all the young-uns worked on it, learning a work ethic that could not be duplicated anywhere else. There was also a picture of her four hound dogs, whom she cherished like her children. Another favorite photo depicted Henrietta sitting in front of the Thomas S. Easly School, surrounded by the staff and all the students.

Every year, she had made sure to take this picture and gave each student's family a framed copy of it at Christmas time. She was so proud of her school. It was the first school at which she herself had taught. She loved it. After twenty years, they asked her to be principal, and she had graciously accepted.

She only knew this one school throughout her entire career. It was around the corner from her home, and in her younger years, she'd walk to school. There were numerous pictures from all of their vacations around the world. There was also a picture of Henrietta and Augusta Blackmoore sitting together having tea under the oak trees, Spanish moss blowing in the wind behind them.

Augusta was the first teacher Henrietta hired, and they became the best of friends. She always admired everything about Augusta. Even though she was a humble woman, Augusta was always neat, clean, put together, and accessorized—boy, could she match things. Henrietta admired the way she lived: her parenting skills, her teaching skills, her talents, the way she dressed, and her children. The only subject they disagreed about was religion. Henrietta was a member of the only true religion, as she put it: the Baptist Church. She attended the Abundant Life Baptist Church, and was buried from that church, as was Becky Sue. Henrietta would tell her parents they made the right choice when it came to the Baptist Church.

There was no such thing as separation of church and state in the South. Here, they played by different rules. They had the American flag hanging in the classroom, and they said the pledge of allegiance daily. They had the South Carolina flag and the Confederate flag both hanging outside on the flagpole. They sang "America the Beautiful" and "Dixie." Mrs. Calhoun was always ready to discuss religion with you, even inside the school! She used to ask Augusta, "When are y'all gonna come to your good senses? How can you be so smart and not know the true church? Girl, I have tried and tried to teach y'all what is right, and girl, you just ain't listening.

I have invited y'all so many times, and y'all just ignore me. What IS your problem, Mrs. Augusta Blackmoore? Lordy, Lordy, sometimes I just don't get y'all!" Augusta would just smile and drink her tea, nodding her head at everything Henrietta said.

She was the closest thing to having a sister. Henrietta had four brothers. Her daddy adored her being the only girl. He had big plans for her, and expected her to become a doctor or a lawyer. He was noticeably disappointed when she announced she would be a teacher. At least she hadn't chosen to be an actress.

Each day, her father would bring her something special. She remembered this happening since she was two. Sometimes it was just a flower, or a trinket; other times it was a big baby doll. But he never forgot. When he came home, she would run into his arms and ask, "What did you bring me, Daddy?" He would say, "All my love," and she would wrestle with him till he opened his hands and revealed a surprise just for her.

She was the oldest child; her first brother had died in childbirth. The third child, a boy, joined the family when Henrietta was three. Needless to say, she was quite spoiled, and was known to pull the new baby out of her mom's bed so she could cuddle with her momma. She just didn't understand. She was used to getting all the attention, and now she had to learn a new behavior: sharing. Well, after four brothers, she learned to share everything—but she was always better at everything than they were. She could shoot better, ride better, work harder, and dance better than all of them, and told them so daily. "I am better than you at everything, and don't you forget it!" She was willing, however, to teach them anything at all; all they had to do was ask. She was such a good teacher.

The one love that Augusta and Henrietta shared was the love of reading. They had each owned an extensive collection of children's books. In fact, both Augusta and Henrietta had been reading to the kindergarten students when the fire broke out.

Once a week, they would have reading marathons. They would compete with each other to see how many books they could read to the children. (I remember taking a class at the University, called Kiddy Lit. We had to read one hundred children's books to get an A, and I did it. I did so love that class.) They would debate between them which were the best books. Henrietta loved *The Little Match Girl*, and read it to the class every Christmas. She cried more than the kids, but they loved the story, too. She also adored *The Princess and the Pea*, which became one of the children's favorites. *Charlotte's Web* and *The Snow Queen* were also at the top of the list, along with *Where the Red Fern Grows* and *The Yearling*. Augusta loved these as well as *The Emperor's New Clothes, Rapunzel, The Spider and the Fly, Guess How Much I Love You?, Frog and Toad are Friends, and Oh, The Places You'll Go*. Between them, they had quite a selection to choose from.

The students loved listening to Henrietta and Augusta as they put on accents and disguised their voices to make the experience dramatic. I'm sure the competition between the two of them was fierce, which would have made it even more exciting. Henrietta really wanted to be an actress, but that was not an approved occupation for a lady of her standing, and her father,

Jasper Grady Calhoun, forbade it. So she did the next best thing: she became a teacher, so she could act in her classroom every day.

This reminded me of myself. I constantly wore costumes in class, dressing up as Galileo when I taught astronomy, Einstein during physics, even Madame Curie for the heck of it. It made class so exciting. I had the largest costume box (I mean trunk) in history. Many of my students would come to my class after school and ask for help with costumes and makeup . . . and not just at Halloween! I eventually took on the role of drama teacher after school, and coached class plays and musicals. I already had the costumes and makeup, and had so much fun that it was a natural transition for me.

Henrietta was a kind and generous woman who would share everything she owned with anyone who needed it. Many a night, people of the town or their families would stay at her house for a variety of reasons. Sometimes they were visiting; sometimes they had lost power; and sometimes they had no home. You could always count on Henrietta. Now that her children were grown and her husband had passed, she had plenty of room.

She had only one other person living with her. Maybelle had lived there for forty-eight years and performed a variety of tasks over that time, from cooking to cleaning to childcare. She had been like a member of the family, but now she was family. Her last job had been simply to keep Henrietta company. Henrietta's extended family told Maybelle that she could live there as long as she wanted, now that Henrietta had joined Samuel in Heaven.

Maybelle was so forlorn, she said she just wanted to go to Heaven with Henrietta and return to her Maker. She probably wouldn't live much longer, as she said that her purpose in life was over now.

Henrietta's funeral was lovely. The flowers were among her favorites: pink peonies, pink roses, pink azalea, and pink dogwood interspersed with Southern greenery. All of these could be found on the grounds of her estate. She had lived a long, happy life, and brought happiness to everyone. And everyone came to her funeral: most of the townsfolk, her children, grand-children, and great-grandchildren, and some distant relatives.

The service was long, because the preacher invited anyone to come up and say a few words about Henrietta. People got in line to secure a place so they wouldn't miss their chance to express their gratitude.

The most touching comments were from Memphis Sawyer's dad. Memphis was a five-year-old kindergarten student who had perished in the fire. He was found in the arms of Henrietta, along with three other students who never made it out. Just like the mother she was, she had stayed with these children until the end. I'm sure she comforted them, wrapped her arms around them, sang to them, and walked into Heaven with them.

Henrietta had walked slowly, with a limp and a cane; she probably couldn't get out quickly enough, and with all the smoke and the intensity of the flames, had she stayed with her students and helped them into eternity.

Mr. Sawyer had just finished burying his son, but he said he wouldn't miss Mrs. Calhoun's funeral. He said he had loved Mrs. Calhoun as much as his son did. Memphis had always felt love from the principal, and considered her a granny. Mr. Sawyer thanked her family for lending her to them and letting the children feel so cared for. "Every day, Memphis would share a story about Henrietta with us, his parents, as he walked home from school. He always smiled after seeing her. Thank you, Henrietta, for being with Memphis, then and now. What an exceptional woman to have been able to touch so many children's lives. I know that Heaven is a better place with her there, and I know that all twelve children are there laughing with her, and Mrs. Blackmoore is taking attendance."

The crowd continued to reminisce and file past her coffin for hours, until the final person had paid homage.

The next day, on the other side of town, Augusta Blackmoore was honored at her funeral. She was being buried from the other church: the Pendleton Street Presbyterian Church. This was also the church that had handled the services for Alden Boone, one of the kindergarteners who had died in the fire.

Augusta was a dedicated teacher, born and raised in Easly. She had never left town, and had no desire to do so. She was content to be a teacher and mother in her hometown. Unlike Henrietta Calhoun, she came from a poor family, but that hadn't affected her teaching or her grandeur. The students loved her and related to her. She had taught generations of the same family in her fifty-five-plus years of teaching. She was also the only one to graduate from high school and college in her family. Her dream was to become a teacher—and she lived her dream. Her students adored her. She was a wonderful kindergarten teacher, the best in the county.

I knew that she wouldn't let her students be frightened, alone in the dark, so she stayed with them. Four more students were found with her shielding their bodies. The remaining five children were found near the doorway and staircase, all huddled together, holding hands. Becky Sue was one of these five. I was glad they were not alone. I was glad they felt some comfort. I prayed they all fell asleep from the smoke and peacefully drifted into Heaven.

Augusta's husband and three children silently cried, and spoke such beautiful words of love for her. Her husband said very few people on this earth perform their job for years and love every minute of it. Very few people feel the love she received from her students, faculty, and family. And very few people get to be married to someone you love so much, it hurts terribly—unbearably—to lose them.

Augusta was a private woman, but she had opened up to Henrietta. She felt safe with her. She shared her fears and dreams with her friend. She worried about leaving her children and husband alone. Well, at least that happened when they were older and out on their own. Although Jamison Blackmoore never got over the loss of his wife, he remained in Easly until he died. She had been his world. They were together over fifty years.

Very few people knew that Augusta had a teacup collection that she had gathered together over the years. She cherished it. She never really left Easly, but lived vicariously through her children and friends. Each time one of them visited a new area or destination, they would bring back a teacup for her. These were very special to her. She would use them for her nightly tea. She didn't believe in saving things for the right time. She said to use them now, because you don't know what tomorrow brings. I'm glad she let her family drink tea from them, because now they would have a fond memory to hold dear. Augusta said memories make a great pillow for old age. This was Augusta Blackmoore.

On the same side of town, the Penley twins, Bonnie and Callie, were laid to rest—a double tragedy. The All Saints Episcopal Church held the services for the twins along with those for Kent Austin. Imagine losing both your daughters at the same time. It was definitely more than her parents could handle. They did not stay together; shortly after the funeral, they each went their separate ways. This often happens with the death of a child.

My mom said you cannot fathom the loss of losing a child. She lost two; I would have had two more brothers. She said those days were the worst of her life. She blamed herself for a long time—a common reaction among parents who have lost their children.

The last funerals were held privately, as the families couldn't bear to deal with their grief publicly. They were for Olivia Jefferson and Grady Mason, both members of the Easly United Methodist Church, which put them to rest. And Billy DeLuke and Memphis Sawyer were buried from the Lutheran Bible Church. May they all rest in peace.

It was determined that both Mrs. Calhoun and Mrs. Blackmoore had been reading to the children, and when the fire broke out, they didn't have a chance to escape, so they stayed with them. The other five were on their way to another class, and they were waiting for a teacher to fetch them near the classroom door. And the four that escaped were upstairs attending an art class. That was the closest description we had then, although the investigation was not over yet.

CHAPTER 23

Becky Sue's Funeral

I WAS COMPELLED TO VISIT the Belmont home after the fire. I knocked on the door, and her younger brother Thomas answered. "Hi, Miss Billie, how y'all doin'?"

I replied, "How are you doing?"

"Y'all want to talk to my momma and daddy?"

"Yes, please."

Becky's parents entered the room, somber and quiet. Fear, sadness, and doubt shadowed their faces. I just didn't know what to say. I held them in my arms, and we all wept for a long time. What can you say? You cannot say, "I know how you feel," because you don't know how they feel. You can't say, "She's in a better place," because how can an innocent five-year-old need to go to a better place? You say you're sorry, but what does that mean? You talk about how the good die young, and see their hollow eyes and know they don't believe that.

I said, "She was the most beautiful young girl, and she made everyone happy. That was because of you. Because you loved her, and she knew it. I cannot imagine how awful this is for you. I don't know how you are dealing with this tragedy. I only know that Becky Sue is smiling down on you, and looks forward to the day you will all be reunited in Heaven. I imagine that Heavenly Father has brought her to her relatives, where she is getting reacquainted with grandparents, cousins, aunts, uncles, her brother, and new friends. They are sharing stories and memories and laughing and loving. She misses you all, but she knows the plan. She knows that when she came to this earth, she didn't know how long she'd be here. She only knew that she had to spend her time learning and loving, and when she was called back, she would go willingly. She promised that she would be happy and share that happiness with everyone, and she did. I know we don't understand. We ask, 'Why? Why her? Why now?' And I don't know why. I only know that I trust God that He knows why. I believe that one day, we will comprehend, and until then, we just have to have faith. There are no words, no explanations, no excuses, no solutions. There is only love and forgiveness."

"Well, we don't understand, and we are angry, sad, and upset with everything and everyone," said Mr. Belmont. "We don't know what to do or how to do it. We've never had to do this before. We don't believe like you do. We've lost faith in God. Why would He let this happen?"

"That's why I'm here. I want to help you. Let me help you pay for the funeral, pick out some clothes, talk to the undertaker, and please, please let me speak at her funeral."

Mrs. Belmont said, "I don't know what to do. I don't know what to say to anyone. I just can't believe this has happened. Who can I blame? I hate everyone. I hate all those parents whose children are still alive. Why did they deserve to live, and not Becky Sue? I hate all those children. I just want to hit someone."

"You can hit me." I stood up and walked over to her and wrapped my arms around her. At first she beat her fists against my chest, and then she sobbed and sobbed uncontrollably. So did Mr. Belmont. I let them cry as long as they needed to. They needed to get it out and talk to someone. I felt so badly for all the parents of the twelve children, but especially for the Belmonts. They just couldn't do anything. They were paralyzed.

I asked, "Shall I come back in the morning, and we can talk about your plans?"

"No, no, we have to start planning now. It's been three days. I know we need to do something," said Mr. Belmont.

"I can't do anything, I just can't," said Mrs. Belmont.

"Please, let me do it. The Calhouns have donated gravesites in their family plot, and offered to pay for anyone who needs help with the funeral costs."

"Help? Who has money for a five-year-old's funeral? No one thinks you'll need it for your child. We are so unprepared."

"We can take care of everything. Let's pick out her prettiest dress to wear and a matching bow for her hair," I gently suggested.

Mrs. Belmont finally agreed.

"I'll be back tomorrow to help. Now please try to rest tonight." I closed the door and cried all the way to the undertaker's. How can you even be an undertaker? How can you stand the pain? How do you sleep at night? When I was in college, there was a job opening for makeup artist at a funeral home in my town. I applied for the job because I was great with makeup, and I wanted to help the deceased to look good. I always felt a special relationship with the dead. When I told my mom, she forbade it. She said, "You cannot live here and work there."

I asked "Why not?"

She said, "You will always smell of the dead."

When I knocked on the undertaker's door, Sam answered, introduced himself as the undertaker, and stood there, looking dead himself. He was exhausted— and beside himself. He said this was the worst event he had ever had to deal with. He looked completely drained. He told me he hadn't slept or eaten in days. He didn't know if he could finish, and he said he would probably retire after these funerals were completed. Although there were three undertakers from surrounding towns who had volunteered to help, he still couldn't wrap his head around it at all. How could all this have happened? How was he going to able to make these children look like themselves, like beautiful little angels? He was good at what he did, but could he be that good? He felt a special obligation to help all these families. He had known them for years. He knew everyone in town.

I said I had come to bring Becky Sue's outfit to wear.

He started to cry, and said, "I've tried so hard to make her look beautiful, and she doesn't look like that sweet little girl I knew."

"May I see her, please?"

"Prepare yourself. I'm still trying."

"Okay, I will." I walked into the room where she lay. He was right; she didn't look like Becky Sue. She had on a long, dark brown wig which tried to imitate her beautiful long curls. The makeup was so thick covering her burned skin that it didn't look like her; it looked like a mask. It was cracking in places. I thought to myself, I must convince the Belmonts to have a closed coffin after they say their goodbyes. I actually hoped they didn't want to see her like this, that maybe they'd want to remember her as she was. But I knew that everyone needs closure to be able to go on. Well, now what? Should I tell Sam he has done a good job? Do I tell the Belmonts so they can be prepared? I prayed that I would know what to say. Her funeral was in two days. No amount of time could fix Becky Sue.

I said goodnight to Sam and walked slowly, ever so slowly, to my car, and then I threw up. I paused for a while looking up at the stars, the heavenly stars, and asked God, "Why?" I knew there would not be an answer tonight. I pleaded with Him to help me say the right words to Becky's parents, knowing the only thing they would recognize would be her dress.

I drove home and reflected upon my own father's death. I had been young, only thirty-nine, and my mom was a mere sixty. She was devastated. She had just retired so she could spend time with my dad. He wasn't well.

They planned to buy a place in Florida and vacation there as much as possible.

I was living out of state, and it was July. I had plans to live and teach in Munich, Germany the coming school year. The deal was, the German teacher would live in my condo and teach German, and I would live in her condo and teach English. I was excited. I called my family to tell them of my plans. On July 6, I was getting ready for the move. I had cleaned out a portion of my condo, confirmed my flight reservations, and was starting to pack.

I was saying my morning prayers, and was told distinctly to go home. I asked why, and my answer wasn't what I wanted to hear. My dad was very sick, and I needed to go right away. I changed my plans, canceled my flight to Germany, booked a flight to my hometown. I called my mom and said I was coming home. I flew out the next morning. It was July 7.

My dad was advised to have exploratory surgery. He checked into the hospital on July 18. On July 19, he had the surgery, and the results weren't good. He had cancer. He was seventy-eight—too young to die. I remember going into the ladies' room in the hall and kneeling on the hard, cold floor and begging the Heavenly Father to save this man. He made it through the night, and I was optimistic. He was good for eight days and I thought he'd come home, but then he had a relapse and got very bad. The prognosis was dim.

I didn't want to prepare for his death, but I knew it was inevitable. This would be the first major death in our family. We'd been through the deaths of grandparents and older aunts and uncles, but this was my dad. I knew I had to be strong for my mom.

On August 7, at 3:30 in the morning, my dad passed away. I was the first one to see him dead in the hospital. My mom cried. We both cried. We hadn't expected this outcome. Mom held him in her arms and commented that his body was the straightest he had ever been in his thirty years of crippling arthritis. We stayed a long while and talked to him, hugged him, and kissed him. He was warm to the touch.

We gathered his belongings and left. It was done. I was the first one to see him in the coffin. I will never forget his image. I was the first one to see Becky Sue dead, and I will never forget that image, either.

I had to be the one to bring his clothes to the under-taker. I was the one to help plan his funeral, and I was the one to go to the funeral parlor and take the limo home to pick up my mom, my brothers, and their families. I got to spend some time with my dad alone as he lay there smiling. He just looked asleep, that's all. I kept thinking, "I wish I could wake him. I wish I could wake up and know that it was all a dream." I was glad he looked so good for my mom's sake.

My dad, my hero, was gone; but I would always remember him. I still talk to him all the time, and he influences me daily. What would he tell me to say to Becky's family? What comfort could I give them? My dad had looked like my dad. He was handsome and whole. He looked so peaceful. Becky didn't look like any of the above. My dad would say, "Tell them she is not there; she is with God. She is still beautiful, and very peaceful. She is happy. She just left a shell of herself behind on this earth. Her body is perfected in Heaven. She is whole and happy. Remember that, and remember her that way." Thanks, Dad. That's what I will share with them. It will still be very difficult, but I know what to say.

The next day, I went over to the Belmonts and shared with them the message my dad had given me. It went better than I thought. They were calmer than the day before, but they hadn't seen Becky Sue yet. I went with them to the funeral parlor, and it was horrible. Mrs. Belmont screamed when she saw Becky Sue. Her husband had to hold her up so she wouldn't collapse on the floor, and was strong for both of them.

As time passed, they were able to calm down, talking about how wonderful she was and how happy she had made them feel. Even Sam told stories of Becky Sue, and they all smiled and chuckled a little. They decided not to let her siblings see her, and to have a closed coffin. My prayers were answered. It was the best thing to do.

Now we had to make it through the funeral. I did get to speak at Becky's funeral, and I echoed the sentiments of all those attending. She was pure joy, and would never be replaced. I paid my last respects and took a break to get ready for the next funeral, which was next in the same church. There was a third funeral across town. Then I would be done for the day. Three funerals in one day was incomprehensible.

CHAPTER 24

After the Funerals: The New School

WELL, WE FINISHED THE FUNERALS. Then we had to try to put the town back together and help the living go on living—an unimaginable task to accomplish. But the people were strong and resilient. We wanted these children to know we would always love them, remember them, and carry on. They would never fade from our memories. A memorial was planned, a statue donated, a plaque created; money was raised, and the school was refurbished.

The statue depicted two older women seated in rocking chairs reading from large storybooks with twelve students clustered around their feet, listening intently with wide-open eyes and smiling faces. It was just the way we wanted to remember them all: joyous and learning. The town had voted, and that was the image they wanted to use as a remembrance of their loved ones. The parents of seven of the students decided to accept the Calhouns' generous offer, and buried their children in the Calhoun plot. The town also voted to place the statue in the cemetery. The other five chose to either bury their children privately or to leave town completely. A bronze plaque with the names of all those who perished was mounted on the school.

How do you cope with such a loss? I still had nightmares about the fire, and so did many others. The only way was to keep busy working on the new school and planning a memorial. It would take years, but we would do it. After grieving and school vacation, we relocated into the grange building. Mrs. Baxter, the assistant principal, became the principal. She was perfect. I knew it was difficult for her to try to replace Mrs. Calhoun, but she tried her best. The mood was somber, and some students had difficulty learning, studying, and focusing, as did some of the teachers. We continued to try, believing that the fallen students would want us to carry on.

The plans for the school were voted upon by the town, and passed unanimously. After the vote, the town council decided that we would use the same plot of land and rebuild the old school, with the exception of the kindergarten room. The new school provided a new space on the first floor, with plenty of large windows and areas to play in. We chose bright colors to paint all the walls, and named rooms after each of the deceased. The library was now called the Henrietta Calhoun Library. The media room, auditorium, and all-purpose room was to be called the Augusta Blackmoore Media

Center. There were twelve rooms, each designated in honor of one of the deceased students.

We loved the project and made frequent trips to watch the progress. The student body, along with the faculty, facilitated several field trips to contribute to the project. On one such day, we planted hundreds of tulip bulbs around the school in honor of the deceased. On another, we cleaned up specific areas, removing building supplies and debris. We also had a picnic and played around the school grounds, like we had done in the olden days before the tragedy. Each and every one of us felt that we were contributing to the new atmosphere that surrounded the building. We planned to be back in the building within two years. Enough time would have elapsed to soften our hearts and minds.

The local businesses contributed to the progress, and everyone came to help in one way or another. Some of the single moms brought food for the workers on a consistent basis. Many fathers came in the evenings or on weekends to contribute their talents and effort. The mayor declared a day of recognition for everyone we had lost. The governor even came to our town three times to offer condolences and work parties to help. He organized everything. We had enough school supplies—more than we'd ever had. New furniture filled the grange. We used it before we moved into our new building. We were truly making progress—it was evident.

We did lose several families. Three families who had lost their children left the town, and at least four others decided to leave and start fresh in a new town. This was my home now. I did debate whether to leave, but I felt comfortable here. I felt needed here. I felt safe here. Most of all, I felt loved here. I carried on as the aide/custodian/helper, and performed whatever jobs were needed. The teachers still valued my scientific knowledge and ability to work with children. I still loved teaching the kids after school. It helped fill a void in all our lives. I still lived in the little cabin behind the school, and welcomed every aspect of my life.

It's very interesting how many parents came to pick up their students after school. You could see the gratitude in their eyes, knowing that they still had their children. In the past, or BTF (before the fire), kids had walked home; now they were mostly joined by parents who kissed them more and hugged them tighter. It seemed to be one of the good results we experienced after the fire. People were more respectful to each other in the town than ever before. There was less bickering and actual fighting. People helped each other more.

I wondered how long this change would last. I hoped that this newfound love and generosity would be the new way of living in Easly. We all felt the change, and welcomed it. With each new day, we saw more progress: not just in rebuilding, but in our lives in general. People suggested activities in which the town as a whole participated regularly. On Sundays, we gathered for potluck dinners, rotating between the various churches. Once a month, there was a family fun night for everyone to enjoy. It usually consisted of a movie shown outside on the wall of one of the buildings in town, homemade root beer, and treats of every kind imaginable. Everyone brought something. For the first time in over a year, we started to smile and laugh.

We could talk about our loved ones who had passed without becoming hysterical. We could tell stories and tales about them and smile. It wasn't easy, but it was happening.

The change was monumental. There was a shift in the entire town from darkness to a tiny glimmer of light, which continually grew brighter and brighter. We now knew that we were going to make it. We could rebuild not only our school and our town, but also— most importantly—our hearts.

It felt so good. Children were learning again, not only learning but enjoying school again. Parents were happier, less fearful, willing to risk letting go of the past, and looking forward to the future. We all decided to try our very hardest.

The school was nearly completed, and we had an open house. Everyone came; TV stations even covered the opening. They wanted to be part of the transformation and celebration, and to wish us well. We wondered how difficult it would be to move back into the old school. Some folks felt it was eerie. Others felt that angels were watching. I didn't feel the actual presence of anyone. I just felt good and peaceful, as if we had been given a blessing.

Several of the clergy spoke and blessed the building, asking the good Lord to watch over us and keep us safe. The mayor spoke, and so did Mrs. Baxter, the new principal. She honored Mrs. Calhoun and Mrs. Blackmoore and mentioned each child by name, commenting on each of their individual talents, who was the best reader, who was the best athlete, who was the kindest, etc. She also talked about what each one of them had added to our lives. The parents quietly sniffled and the teachers and guests all agreed, nodding their heads in unison.

Together, they unveiled the bronze plaque for all to see. It had been donated by the townspeople collectively. It listed the names of the fourteen people who had perished that day in the school fire. It was mounted onto the facade of the building, so everyone could see it. Some people still felt that the building should have been razed and a park constructed in its place. Others were comfortable with renovating the old building, but adding more safety features and fire sprinklers, and moving the kindergarten to the first floor. I agreed that these necessary changes made the original building acceptable to the building department, the fire department, and to us, which was most important.

Many things were the same about the building and the school day, but many were different. The rooms seemed the same except for fresh paint and new furnishings. There was a good feeling when you walked into the rooms, which pleased me greatly. I knew that sometimes, when you enter a room or a house that is haunted or has the presence of spirits, there can be an obvious feeling—sometimes good, sometimes bad. But not here; it felt okay.

I toured each and every room, even the basement, and felt nothing. Thank God. But it was different. We missed those who had passed. We quoted them as if they were still with us. One teacher said to another, "Let's ask Mrs. Calhoun's opinion about that particular book," and then realized what she had said. Both smiled with tears in their eyes. This was all normal.

Students talked about some of the students who had passed, and it evoked sad feelings in the room. At the same time, it was wonderful to talk about them. I myself still had a difficult time talking about Becky Sue. It was just too painful still. This would change with time. As my mom said, this horrific event would teach me new things, and I must learn from them. And I did. She was always right; I didn't learn that until later in life.

After the presentation, the applause was endless, and we were all happy.

Move-in day was a week away. We still had lots to do with decorating, organizing, and cleaning; but the rooms were painted, and the furniture, supplies, and books were in place. We were ready! Mrs. Baxter had decided that we would have an assembly on the first day to welcome everyone back to the school, and to introduce the new faces.

There were five new kindergarteners, three of whom were siblings of students who had passed. We thought it might be especially difficult for them, but little children are so accepting and flexible, and they seemed to adjust better than we did. One little girl proudly announced that she was a sister of Olivia Jefferson, who had died in the fire. "I miss her, but I know she'll help me in school." And then there was the brother of Grady Mason. He didn't want to talk about his dead brother, as he referred to him. And then there was the brother of Memphis Sawyer, who had adored Mrs. Calhoun. His name was Otis, and he said he was sad that Mrs. Calhoun wouldn't be his principal. His daddy said she was a fine lady, but that Mrs. Baxter was a nice lady, too. We were hopeful that all would return to normal—whatever normal was now.

My friend Jonathan was ever-present to help me, support me, and love me. He was very quiet, letting me grieve and handle things the way I felt best, but he was always there: sometimes by my side, sometimes in the shadows, but there. I truly appreciated the fact that I could count on him his advice, his help, and even his silence. He suggested that during the first school break we get away for a little R&R, which sounded great to me. It was good to plan something happy instead of a funeral.

Jonathan had dealt with the death of his wife from breast cancer. It had been long and terrible, so he knew what it felt like to experience tragedy. He always had a great attitude. He said he cherished every day the Lord gave him. He was filled with gratitude for even the smallest things on earth. That was just one of the reasons I loved him. I had hoped that we could eventually be more than a couple. He had talked about marriage. I was reluctant, considering that I had two failed marriages already; but now it sounded good, real good. I liked that phrase. I heard parents use it often: "My children, they good, they real good." They would frequently leave out verbs when they spoke. The language and the colloquialisms were endearing to me, and so were the Southern people.

CHAPTER 25

My Mom

MY MOM, MY GREATEST CHEERLEADER, was always there for me. She calmed the rage inside me. She supported me. She helped me survive. She never gave up on me and would defend me to the death. She was a strong woman. She had to be. She had learned at an early age that she would have to take care of herself.

Born into a large family during the Depression, Nelly learned to survive. She had ten brothers and sisters, and they all helped on the farm. My grandmother had to milk the cow, feed the chickens, and feed twelve hungry mouths every day. That in itself was a miracle. Each of the children had chores to do around the house, starting when they were three years old.

At three, Mom fetched wood for the kitchen wood-burning stove, which was also the only heat source in the house, so that Grammy could cook for the day. My mom's chores advanced as she grew. At four, she was feeding the animals, and at five, she had to walk to the stream and fetch a big bucket of water for the day's activities before she even walked to school. One day, she sloshed more water on her socks and shoes than she actually carried into the kitchen. She had no time to change, even if there had been another pair of clean socks to be found.

It was the Depression, and they had very little of anything. She shared socks and undies with her older sisters, whether they fit or not, and learned to wear socks as mittens in the winter. All of these experiences taught my mom to be the strongest woman I knew. She tried to teach me these lessons, but I was spoiled, and didn't take well to her trying to curb my activities and spending.

Her mom, Nelly, said, "We always had food with chickens and eggs, and a cow and milk and vegetables from the garden." My grandmother was the original pioneer woman and could teach self-reliance to anyone. Nelly prided herself on never missing school, or even being tardy. In fact, she had perfect attendance throughout her school years, even walking through a snowstorm one day—only to have the janitor tell her school was canceled and to go home.

The day my mother spilled the water, her teacher noticed her wet shoes and socks, and instructed her to dry them on the radiator. She probably thought she was stupid. She didn't know the extent of the chores she was responsible for at such an early age. Nelly was obedient, however, and did as she was instructed. She never thought anyone would think poorly of her. Why would she? She hadn't been raised that way, and she thought everyone thought like she did. She was gullible in that way. I, too, believed that everyone was good at heart, and thought the way I did. Boy, was I wrong! There were many dishonest people with evil hearts and ulterior motives who didn't believe anything I believed.

One of the most important lessons my mom taught me was to give everyone the benefit of the doubt, because you don't know what they are going through. She said everyone was going through their own personal tragedy on a daily basis, and we should be kind. She also said, "Don't expect anything, and you will never be disappointed." She had learned this the hard way. She was passed over for a scholarship, and, later in life, a job promotion. She also learned she had to protect herself. When she ran for class president in ninth grade, she lost by one vote. My mom thought the correct thing to do was to vote for other opponent, which she did, and she lost by that one vote. This didn't taint her; it educated her. My mother taught me to be kind and to love people, but to also be cautious and remember who I was. During this ordeal, I forgot who I was—along with my value and self-worth.

Her mom spent her entire day taking care of the children, the house, the animals, the meals, and her husband. There was little time for niceties or private time with her children. She would tell me that she admired her own mother, because every night, she had a meal on the table for twelve people. She also made sure there was breakfast, and the children came home for lunch, too. Mind you, she was also nursing a baby as she did everything else.

What a rough life; but, as my mom would say, "We never knew we were poor, because we always had food, and during the Depression, some folks didn't have food. Nelly's father, "Grandpa," or "Ta," as we called him, said we didn't have to wait in those lines and take free food, we'd make do." They always survived. Grammy had no time to teach my mom to cook. She would tell her to watch, but she couldn't touch, because if she spoiled the food or did something wrong, there would be no dinner. Well, she must have watched really well, because she became a gourmet cook. She tried to teach me, but I had other ideas.

In first grade, my mom survived a test that would shape her entire life to come. At the end of the school year, she and another student were told they would have to remain in the first grade and repeat it because there were not enough chairs or desks in the second grade. She knew she wasn't dumb; she hadn't done anything wrong. They just randomly chose two students. What a lawsuit this would be today. Imagine No Child Left Behind. She was hurt and wondered why the teacher had done this to her. She made up her mind that she would be the smartest student in the class and the best reader in the school, which she did and was. At the end of the school year, they promoted her to third grade— she completely skipped the second grade.

She continued to excel and got straight As in all her classes, reading voraciously every day. She would walk to the library and come home with as many books as they would let her check out. She thought, *How wonderful, I can go anywhere and be anyone when I read.* At night, she used a kerosene lamp to read and study by.

I know who I am. She taught my brothers and me to "always remember you are a child of God; you come from kings. Now straighten your crown and carry on." She believed in being kind to everyone and honest with your fellow man.

She also believed in standing up for yourself and defending what was true and right. She said that in the end, it would all work out. If it hadn't worked out yet, then it wasn't the end yet. At the age of ten, she wanted religion, so she walked down to the local church and asked a nun to baptize her, and the priest did. She was innovative, powerful, and bold. She knew who she was.

And at twelve, she experienced one of her first tragedies. She and her best friend Violet went to the local quarry to gather tadpoles for a science project. They were leaning over the jagged rocks and reaching into the water to scoop them out. It was getting dark, and Nelly told Violet she had to go home. She tried to persuade her to follow, but Violet said, "Just a couple more," as she climbed higher and perched himself precariously on a jagged ledge. That was the last time my mom saw her friend alive. She apparently slipped into the water and drowned. The police came to interview my mother because she was the last person to have seen her alive. They lived near each other, and had walked home from school together daily. Nelly's older brother, a champion swimmer, had to retrieve her body. It was so tragic. Violet's family never recovered, and moved away that summer.

Nelly was no stranger to death. One of her other classmates had rheumatic fever, and she would bring him his homework after school. One day, when she went to visit, she looked in the window and saw that he was dead on the porch. She was curious and sad, and wondered why young children had to die. She also learned at an early age that her sister Nellie had died at the tender age of three from scarlet fever. My mom looked like her, and her father always loved her and felt she was a special angel that God sent after they lost Nellie. One day, her mom said Nellie appeared in the kitchen all dressed in white beside the wood-burning stove, with her long blonde curls and a big white bow fastened in her hair. Her mother had always placed a big white bow in her hair. She knew it was Nellie, and it gave her great comfort to see her for a brief moment. She did not speak. She only smiled, and then she was gone.

My mom was born three years after Nellie's death. She became strong as these events shaped her life and prepared her for her own future tragedies. Over the course of her life, she buried two babies, her mom, her dad, her husband, five sisters, four brothers, one sister-in-law, and one brother-in-law. That is a lot of death to endure. And she was responsible for handling nine of their funerals.

She also became a top athlete. (I certainly didn't take after her in this area.) She won the medal of honor in athletics. Whatever she participated in, she did to the hundredth degree. She taught my siblings and I that if you're going to be involved in something, give 100 percent of yourself. She should have been the dean of a women's college—she was perfect for that occupation. In her senior year, she received a scholarship, but wasn't able to go and receive it. There was no money to take a train or any other transportation. It was the

Depression. This saddened her, but again, she straight-
ened her crown and went on to find work and help her
mom and dad with the bills, donating half her paycheck
to the household. She knew her parents were doing the
best they could.

Her mom never learned to read or write English,
and couldn't defend her or help her. My mom defended
me, though, and helped me always. I felt like she hadn't
gotten her fair share. She deserved more from life. It
was never easy, but she learned more in those formative
years than most people learn in their entire lifetime.

When I was accused of hitting my student, my mom
vehemently opposed my accusers. She wanted to fight
for me. I loved her loyalty, and asked her to pray for me.
I saw her every day, and she consoled me and reminded
me who I was again and again.

My mother never really fulfilled her dreams, but she
fell in love with her boss at the local grocery store. She
was sixteen, and applied for a job. He said he wanted to
hire her, but there was no ladies' room in the store. He
told her to come back in a week, which she promptly did.
He first gave her a tour of the bathroom he had built for
her, and then he hired her. That was my dad—my hero!
How romantic to have someone build a bathroom for
you. It was a great story to tell your grandchildren, as
they say.

Images of my family, especially my mom, flooded
my mind, and whenever I felt like I was lost, forsaken,
or couldn't go on, these images sustained me. Nothing
but the thoughts and images of my loved ones made
any sense anymore. Just a thought or a quick talk on the
phone or a visit to my mom was enough to rejuvenate

me, buoy me up, and help me keep my head above water so I could go on. I spoke to her every day.

My dad was eighteen years older than my mother, and my grandparents vehemently objected to their marriage, but they were in love—true love. My mom had never been off the hill, as they said. She had never traveled or really gone anywhere. My dad loved showing her new places, new food, and new activities. He took her to out to dinner for her first lobster, and laughed watching her eat it. He eventually taught her how.

He took her on her first trip to New York and to her first opera, *La Boheme*. She quickly fell in love with opera, and both my parents adored Luciano Pavarotti. I am so grateful that my parents instilled a love of opera in me. I listen often, and am calmed and fulfilled by its grandeur. Because of them, I have attended many, many operas, and have seen Luciano sing in person twice. So, my little Italian father who looked like a mafioso taught my mom a variety of things in their forty-eight years together, and we, in turn, learned to appreciate many of these.

They finally married with mom's parents' blessing, and left on a honeymoon to Florida. Halfway there, my dad went into anaphylactic shock from eating some seafood in a Southern restaurant. He was driving, and pulled into the first hotel just as his eyes swelled shut. My mom was nineteen, a new bride, and didn't know how to drive. She ran into the lobby and begged the hotel manager to call a doctor, which he did, and tended to him. The doctor said he could have died. They stayed the night, and continued their trip. My innocent nine-teen-year-old mom had almost lost her husband on their honeymoon. This was one of the adventures that made my mom strong. They raised three children, and lost another two. My mother began working at age thirty-six, when we were all quite settled in school.

My dad wasn't well, and we needed the income. At fifty-six, my father lost his job and opened his own business. Within ten years, my mom was taking care of her husband, three children, and her own mother. It was a struggle to take care of everyone and work full time. My brother was divorced, and my mom was now raising her grandson. Soon after my divorce, I moved back home to add to the burden.

My mom is the strongest woman I have ever known. She could make it through any situation and come out with her head held high—and better for it. I wished I was as strong as she was. She tried to give me her strength, and sometimes, it worked. How I wished that I had paid more attention to her when she had tried to teach me the lessons of life. I had trusted too much, believed too much; and now I was suffering. I didn't know it then, but my mom later told me that she cried every night about me right before she prayed for me. She once said she couldn't leave this earth until all her children and grandchildren were settled in life and joyous. I guess she will never die, if those are the conditions.

During my ordeal—for at least six months—I called my mom every day. She always had some words of wisdom. She said I should never give up. I was close to giving up after attending DCF Court. The deck was definitely stacked against me, and I saw no way out. Mom calmly reminded me that it wasn't over. She suggested looking for other employment, and going to the library every day to read the bestsellers and peruse the want ads. I ended up going to a local bookstore to read the bestsellers. I thought, *That's what I'll do. I'll write a book.* When I informed my mom, she said, "Why would you want to do that? Why rekindle those old, dark memories?" It was true. I kept them hidden away.

I had managed to quell them for years, but now I was ready to share and write those memories down for others to read—and maybe learn from. Part of me was scared, and I second-guessed myself. Who would want to read what happened to me? Who cares about what happened? But then, every day, I saw or heard something in the news about a case of false accusation, or a pathetic situation in which someone's life was destroyed or taken from them because of deceit and lies, and I would think, I need to do this. I need to tell my story. I convinced my mom, and now she cheers me on and wishes me the best of luck. Sometimes, she even reads the chapters and critiques them. And sometimes, she even likes what I write.

CHAPTER 26

Adjusting to the New School

It seemed easy at first to adjust to the new school, even though painful memories were recurring. In addition to the daily schedule in place, the principal had added a new routine: a weekly fire drill. I guess it was necessary, but it became tedious after repeated months of practicing the drill. Everyone got used to it, and performed in a satisfactory way. It pleased the principal, the fire department, and the parents, so we continued.

We also continued with our studies, which became exciting again, especially science. During science classes, the teachers let me be a guest teacher and share my knowledge and experience. I loved it—especially the unit on astronomy. I felt like a teacher again. And the best part was that the students came to me again after school for help in science.

The school didn't really participate in a recognized science fair contest, so I decided to start one of our own. It would be held only at our school, and all grades would participate. Each student would choose a topic to research, and create a science-fair board. The teachers, the librarian, and I would help them with research, construction, and participation. I suggested it to Mrs. Baxter, our new principal. She thought it was a great idea, and helped implement it.

We had an assembly at which we discussed the requirements and announced that there would be one prize for each grade level. Nearly everyone thought it would be fun. I was appointed as the chairwoman of the project, which made my heart sing. I met with Mrs. Dixon, the librarian, and she was extremely helpful. At fifty-four, she was one of our youngest faculty members. Mrs. Dixon was filled with innovative ideas for the students, and set up stations in the library to help them. She compiled lists of references, piles of books and data, and numerous pictures and charts. She was ready to help in any way.

I was allowed two hours during the day to meet with students in the library to help them get started. It was exciting and fulfilling. After my cleaning and required chores were completed, I reported to the library to help the students. Since this was all new to everyone, I had to train the teachers and Mrs. Dickson on what to do and expect. We wanted all of the children to participate, so we provided all necessary supplies, including paints, boards, glue, tools, etc. We knew some students had nothing at home, and would need everything. Two hours a day wasn't enough, so I made myself available after school every day for two hours. It worked out well. The students had two months to prepare.

The judges were chosen as follows:

Mr. J. J. Radcliff, who managed the local Piggly Wiggly store, was a fixture in town, and knew everyone and everything about it. No one used his real first name when referring to him. It was always just J.J. Did he even have a first name? He was constantly visible walking through the aisles of the store, and would personally escort you to the location of any item. J.J. held the all-time record for the lowest incidence of pilfering throughout the entire chain of Piggly Wiggly grocery stores. I think everyone liked him so much, they just couldn't steal from him. He had a wife and three children, and made a fine living for his family. They had lived there all their lives. He was so pleased that he had been chosen.

Then there was Mrs. Bea Jacobs, who owned the Honey Bee Bakery. She served some of the best delicacies: hummingbird cake, bread pudding, pecan, sweet potato, and key lime pies, and her famous banana pudding pie, which was her claim to fame. And the national Banana Pudding Festival had started right here in Easly because of her pie! Her goal was to make sure every customer tasted at least one bakery item during each trip to the bakery. This strategy surely increased sales for her, and it most certainly increased the weight of the townspeople. She reminded me of Aunt Bea on The Andy Griffith Show—you know Opie's great aunt. She was a stout little woman with a smile that wrapped around her face; as tall as she was wide, and as jolly as old Saint Nick.

Next was Mr. Clifford Dudley, who owned the Vintage General Store. In fact, his family had owned it since its inception. He had grown up in the family store and knew where every item was located. As a child, he had worked there before school, after school, and on the weekends. Everyone knew that when he grew up, he would be the only one to run the store—and they were right.

"I'm looking for a light bulb, Mr. Dudley."

"Industrial, aisle 3, incandescent, aisle 7, and household, aisle 2."

"Wow, I'm impressed. You really do know where everything is located."

His two older brothers decided to leave Easly and head out for the big city of Columbia to make their fortune. Wesley, his oldest brother, became an accountant after graduating from Clemson. And Crofton, his other brother, settled in Myrtle Beach. He owned a five-and-ten store, and after some time had passed, his beachside real estate was worth a fortune. They had both done very well.

Mr. Dudley even said he'd give a 50 percent discount to any of the students who purchased supplies for their science fair projects at his store. He was so happy to be a part of the team of judges.

Next in the lineup was Mrs. Penny Tillerson. She owned the Mercantile and Penny Arcade and Café. The café served all the favorites: sweet tea, hush puppies, fried okra, and chicken fried steak and biscuits. She said she would cater the awards ceremony for a big discount. She boasted that if you couldn't find an item in her store, then they didn't make it on Earth! Her store supplied the locals with the current fashions, but I didn't know how current they were. At least that was how they were advertised. I think she may have coined the phrase penny arcade. She was a clever woman who capitalized on her creative sales abilities, and she had a lot going on in the store. You could shop, you could eat, or you could play games. All of these different outlets increased her sales. She was a very smart lady.

And finally, we asked Dr. Marshall McClain, our own beloved doctor. He bragged that he had probably delivered most of the students in our school. Everyone loved him. He was the kind of doctor who still made house calls. He also had an interesting hobby: he played the saw. He could make it sing, and often performed at the town talent show. Dr. McClain had outlived two wives, and now, at his age, he was just enjoying his grandchildren and life. He said he would never retire. He'd just die at the hospital someday. We thought we should have at least one person with a scientific background on our committee of judges. He graciously accepted.

The students were more excited about this project than they had been about anything in two years' time… but I was the most excited. The event was my baby, and I wanted it to be successful. I sent a note home to all the parents explaining what the science fair entailed and what was required, and let them know that I would be available after school every day for two hours and that I had many supplies they could use. I bought them at Mr. Dudley's general store (at a 50 percent discount!). All the parents had to do was reserve a time slot. The signup sheet filled up fast, so I also designated a time slot before school for an hour. I was in pig heaven. I felt like I was teaching full time again.

The students' projects were outstanding, thanks to the efforts of Mrs. Delila Dixon and several other teachers. I remember one in particular: Miss Florence Walker. Florence had never married. This wasn't by choice; it just didn't happen. She said she had all the children she needed at school. She spent most of her free time working on school lessons or projects, and was always, always available to help the children. She said the good Lord knew what He was doing. Some of us just had to stay single to help the others with their young-uns.

Her greatest joy was teaching the third grade. She said they were the perfect age to teach: they could read, they were so curious about everything in life, and they laughed at her jokes. They even believed her threats about talking to their parents if they misbehaved. Most impressive, though, was the fact that they wanted to learn! They came to school on time, and willingly.

Miss Walker said it was the only grade in which she witnessed this. Second graders were just starting to read, and were not as curious yet. Fourth graders were starting to be full of themselves, and beyond the fifth grade, they started to get uncontrollable and too independent. She had substituted in all the different grade levels in Greenville during her beginning teaching years, and knew firsthand that she was correct about this particular fact.

Miss Walker had grown up in Greenville and wanted to teach there, but when she landed her job in Easly, she knew it was the right place for her to teach and live. She never left . . . and never wanted to, either. She had begun her career as a third-grade teacher, and hoped to end her career as a third-grade teacher here in Easly, as well.

She was so willing to help the students with their science fair projects. Miss Walker matched my time schedule, and even bought a range of art supplies for the children to use. Science was her favorite subject to teach, just like me. I knew I liked this woman. We got along so well. We shared ideas about scientific theories, discoveries, and future events, and spent hours just discussing science. She had so many ideas about projects to share with the kids.

Mr. Dudley was extremely grateful for the sales that stemmed from the fair. He had higher sales that month than he had experienced in years. Florence even brought homemade dinner for herself, Mrs. Dixon, the librarian, and me. She was a fine cook, and we eagerly gobbled down her gourmet dishes as we worked late after school. With all these positive scenarios, we couldn't help but be a total success! The three of us just melded together. Since we were all single, we didn't have to worry about what time we had to be home, or who would cook dinner. No one was waiting for us, and we could eat out or bring food at our leisure. Some days, we worked and laughed into the wee hours of the morning. And remember, I had all the keys to everything, which was very convenient.

Mrs. Dixon, the best librarian in all the South, was a sweet, kind, gentle soul. She was divorced, and had never remarried. She raised her daughter to be an outstanding citizen in the community: she never caused a problem, and was always obedient.

I loved Mrs. Dixon's teaching style. If a student was involved in anything improper, she would simply walk over to them, stare at them, and say, "UNACCEPTABLE." And that did it. She gave of herself unselfishly. She knew every book in the library, and had probably read every one of them. She also made herself available before and after school to help the students. Her daughter was so influenced by her mom's success that she also became a teacher. She taught in a high school near Columbia, South Carolina. Mrs. Dixon had been a classroom teacher for years before she became a librarian, so she was very familiar with all the techniques and rules of conduct. She was having the time of her life. That is the word: LIFE. There was a new breath of life in the school. I was joyous.

Every night, I called my mom to tell her about the goings-on. I had no time to be sad, forlorn, or stressed. I was the happiest I'd been in over fourteen years. We continued for two months, working on science projects alongside our daily schedules. We met twice with the judges to explain their responsibilities and to show them how to score the projects and interview each student. We were going to award a first-place and second-place prize for each grade level: fourteen prizes in all.

Mrs. Alexandria Wellington, the art teacher, only answered to Mrs. Wellington. She was from Charleston and knew it—and she made sure everyone else knew it, too. She imagined she was related to Scarlett O'Hara. She offered her services in prize creation for the science fair. I didn't know what to expect, but I knew I had to say yes to her offer if I wanted to remain friends with her after the fair. Her image defined a true Southern belle. She certainly dressed the part; the only thing missing was Spanish moss hanging from her arms. I could have sworn she lived with Rhett Butler at Tara. She had even named her first daughter Tara. She sounded like Scarlett, and frequently quoted her. One day, I overheard a student telling her he hadn't finished his art project yet, and without skipping a beat, she replied, "After all, tomorrow is another day." I believed she created situations that were perfect for quoting lines from *Gone with the Wind*. She loved teaching the older students, and referred to the kindergarteners as "a passel of mealy-mouthed brats." Of course, she would never say that to their faces, because she was, indeed, a lady.

On her first date with Captain Dean Wellington, she had said, "That's what's wrong with you. You should be kissed, and often, by someone who knows how." He married her not long after that.

One day, when there was a power outage because everyone in the county was running their swamp coolers, her food was inedible because her refrigeration unit was off. Her reaction? "As God is my witness, I'll never be hungry again."

Mrs. Wellington could be charming and demanding at the same time. Her husband put up with her strange ways because she was always so entertaining, and because he was a little quirky himself. She was a great art teacher, and I had faith that the prizes for the fair would be perfect.

Mrs. Baxter didn't believe in everyone getting a prize, like some schools offered. She said she wanted to prepare her students for the real world. Sometimes you win, sometimes you lose. Learn to deal with it. Next time, try even harder if you didn't get first place. The students knew ahead of time what the requirements were and how they would be scored. It would be a fair contest. We had preened the judges, and they were ready.

We continued to work very hard, and the day arrived for the presentations. The Augusta Blackmoore Media Center was organized with tables and chairs for each student to set up their project board and any experiment equipment they needed. The parents were invited that evening to witness the students' presentations. The judges were equipped with clipboards and a series of questions to ask in order to score the students and their work. The areas scored included: 1. the subject matter; 2. the students' answers to the judges' questions; 3. originality of project and title; 4. the actual board; and 5. their presentation of data. The parents and judges went from student to student, asking questions about their projects, taking notes, and scoring them as they were interviewed. Some of the questions the judges asked were as follows: Where did you get this idea? What research did you do? What was your hypothesis? What did you measure, and how? What does that graph tell you? Who might want to know this information? What was the hardest part, or the most fun, or the most surprising? Who helped you? What would you have done differently? What did you base your conclusion on?

There was such a variety of projects—How Much Weight Can Your Boat Float, A Matter of Time, DNA Fingerprinting, The Swimming Secrets of Duck Feet, The Reasons for the Seasons, Blood Clotting to the Rescue, Rocketology, Craters and Meteorites, Bubbleology,

Measuring the Surface Tension of Water, and more. It was going to be very difficult for the judges to just choose fourteen winners.

The presentations went on for three hours, and at the end, there were light refreshments served from the Honey Bee Bakery. Mrs. Jacobs was so proud. The whole program lasted from 6:00 to 9:00 P.M. Then the judges met together to discuss their findings and the winners. It was difficult, but they narrowed it down.

As I walked around listening to the judges' questions and the perfectly-orchestrated answers the students gave, I was so proud, as if they were my own children. In a way, they were. The memory of Daniel Ray disrupting our science fair presentations surfaced and tried to destroy the moment for me, but I wouldn't let the voice sabotage my feelings. It was so different here and now. The students weren't presenting discipline problems like Daniel and his classmates had done in the past. They were mostly obedient, and glad to be. They sincerely wanted to learn, participate, and win!

I had prepared the students to graciously accept the outcome, and to congratulate the winners and clap, even if they didn't win. They seemed to grasp the concept that not everyone could win, and that they should remain proud of what they had accomplished. I was looking forward to tomorrow's awards assembly. I had my personal favorites, and was curious to see if the judges agreed with me.

It was late when I called my mom. She was happy for me, and shared in my joy. I could always count on her.

Wednesday morning arrived. The parents came again, grateful to accompany their children. The judges were ready, and so was I. Mrs. Baxter began by thanking all who had participated, including the students, the teachers, the librarian, and the judges. Then she said, "We want to especially thank Miss Billie, who spearheaded this wonderful project, and allowed us to flourish and forget sad past memories and concentrate on happier times and today." She began to applaud, and everyone clapped and rose to their feet and gave me a standing ovation. I sat there and cried.

It was all worth it. It was the best science fair show I had ever participated in. All the trophies I had received in the past were meaningless compared to this very moment. The judges announced their winners, and I had chosen six of the fourteen they selected. It actually didn't matter who won, because that day, we were all winners. We were all happy and smiling. I thanked the students, the parents, Mrs. Baxter, and the judges, expressing my gratitude to all of them. So many children ran up to me, thanking me for the experience. We decided that this should be an annual activity, and that I would be in charge every year. And that was just fine with me.

In the spring, I planned the Great Egg Drop, another experiment-driven activity. Each student designed a contraption to hold a raw egg. I would go to the top of the school and drop off the contraptions, and we would witness whose creation kept the egg whole, amidst screams and squeals. This became a favorite activity for everyone—an annual event. It was just wonderful to participate in all this science.

The months passed by, and one day, the principal called me to her office. She said the town had decided to have a memorial service, and the mayor, police chief, and fire chief had decided to honor some heroes and present them with awards for their bravery. I was one of them. I wasn't expecting this, nor did I want it. I had left it all in the past now, and didn't want to dredge it up again; but she insisted that it was proper. I really dreaded this event and wasn't sure if I wanted to participate. Mrs. Baxter said it would make everyone content, especially the parents. They would let me know when this would take place, and until then, I would just carry on as usual. And so I did. I continued to help teach science classes and do my regular job performing my janitorial chores.

One night, as I was locking up the school and securing all the rooms and lights, I had a flashback of Danny Ray yelling at me, "You're gonna lose your job. We're gonna sue." It upset me terribly, and I didn't know what to do about it. That night, I had a nightmare about the fire and Becky Sue dying. For a moment, I thought, "Why didn't Danny Ray die instead of her?" I know that was an awful thing to think, but it was truly how I felt for a long time until I forgave him. Life doesn't always turn out the way you expect. The bad feelings and nightmares continued, so I decided I had to talk to someone about it, especially if I was going to survive going to the memorial service. I decided to ask Dr. McClain to recommend someone.

CHAPTER 27

Counseling

I WANTED SOMEONE who wasn't from Easly. I wanted to see someone out of town, and to be private about it. The doctor told me about a wonderful woman who lived in Greenville, about a half hour from Easly. I called her the next day and made an appointment. I thought I was healed, but according to Coralee, I wasn't. I made regular appointments to see her. It was enlightening and healing. She took me through all the loss again. It was painful. I felt like a failure again about losing my husband, my career, my second husband, my family, and then Becky Sue. She helped me see that these events were in the past, and that I was free of all of it. It was not my fault. I could do what I wanted, and no matter what anyone said, I knew the truth. She taught me forgiveness again. I forgave Danny Ray, his family, Mr. Anderson, God, and myself. It was a long process. She would give me homework each week so I could progress.

Previously, even though William and I had gone to counseling, I still thought people sought out counseling were weak, and failures. There was such a stigma attached to it. I didn't feel that way anymore. In fact, I thought everyone should go to counseling, because everyone has something that they are dealing with and need help with. Each week, I would report back with my homework in hand. It was always a writing assignment to help me grow. She asked me to write a letter to Danny Ray, then to my ex-husband, then to Mr. Anderson, and finally, to myself. After I read them to myself and to her, she had me burn them. I secretly wanted to send the letters to all of these people, but Coralee said that would defeat their purpose. The burning ritual was supposed to help me let it go.

I still hadn't completely forgiven them yet, but I did the writing each week, and talked to her for many hours. Sometimes, I felt like it was hopeless, but at other times, I thought, *I can do this. I'm going to overcome it.* I could feel I was getting stronger. I didn't tell anyone I was going to see Coralee. I felt ashamed. I thought I was weak, and that she was right that I needed more help. I committed to continue to see her until I felt whole again. There were so many areas to cover.

"Did you have a problem with your parents?"

"No, I loved them and got along with them."

"Do you still hold onto your abusive first husband, and the awful way he treated you?"

"Yes, I do."

"Don't you feel that you deserve to be happy?"

William had said that if I ever left him, no one would ever marry me again. He was wrong. Why wasn't

I worthy? Then I thought about my second marriage, which had also ended quite sadly. It wasn't my fault. Maybe it was true I didn't deserve to be happy; but then I thought about Jonathan. He thought I was worthy and deserving and loving, and wanted only good things for me. So I was okay. I knew that if someone could love me, I would make it.

My therapist taught me you should treat everyone as if they are experiencing a tragedy, and 95 percent of the time, you will be correct. She taught me not to measure myself by other people's successes, but to compare myself only with my progress. She said I always set myself up for failure because I compared my weaknesses to other people's strengths. She said to look at how far I'd come in just a short period of time.

She taught me that in order to achieve inner peace, I must learn how to forgive. These were the hardest and most important lessons to learn. I swore that I would learn to forgive. I swore that I would do my daily affirmations, and start each day with prayer and positive thoughts. She taught me that it was okay to grieve. She said to cry when I needed to, to scream, shout, lie on the floor. Sob in the shower. Be still. Run. Walk. Create. Live my truth. Share without fear. Release my pain. Breathe. Be courageous. Throw away the map. Wander. Be real. Be compassionate. Read. Seek friendship. Be vulnerable. Never fear being broken. Even broken crayons still color beautifully. And aren't we all broken? She also said I must be willing to leave the life I had planned in order to find the one that was waiting for me.

The most important thing I gleaned from our sessions was that I had to time my grieving and sadness.

She said I had the right to scream, yell, cry, and vent, but I had to set a timer for ten to fifteen minutes, and when it rang, I had to get up, stop my crying, and do something else. This practice helped me the most, because I had to force myself to do something positive. I began to set the timer less and less, and began to automatically stop by myself.

In the beginning, my bouts of crying were gut-wrenching, body-shaking sobs. There were oceans of tears. My throat hurt from crying, and my voice was hoarse. My eyes looked like scarlet roadmaps. My world went black. My vision narrowed to only a tiny slit of color. The rest was darkness. The crying started immediately. Eventually, I experienced different ways to grieve, but there were never stages. I cried myself awake. I cried myself to sleep. I mostly cried in the car, where no one could hear me. I cried driving to the store, and in the store. I also cried a lot in the shower, where my sounds were muffled by the rushing water. I cried. I cried often and a lot, and didn't give a damn how much, or who heard me. I was angry with anyone who questioned why and how long I cried. It is different for everyone and every situation. There is no timeline for grieving. It takes everyone a different amount of time and a different method to survive. Don't let anyone tell you to stop and move on. Only you will know when to proceed.

I read somewhere that grief is really just love. It's all the love you want to give, but cannot. All that unspent love gathers up in the corners of your eyes, the lump in your throat, and in that hollow part of your chest. Grief is just love with no place to go. I've also learned that grief really never ends, whether it is a loss of a person, job, a career, or a marriage. It just changes. It's a passage. It is not a place to stay, nor is it a sign of weakness or lack of faith. Rather, it is a sign of love. I've also learned that when I am sorrowful, I look in my heart and see the truth, which is that I am weeping for that which was my delight. How blessed I was to have the things that are now absent from my life. Some never experience any of them.

Each morning as I mourned, I realized that it is a reawakening that things were different now. Coralee said if I held on too tightly to the past, I wouldn't be able to grasp the future. I was learning to let go. It was a very slow process. William Wordsworth said it best: "Though nothing can bring back the hour of splendor in the grass, of glory in the flower; we will grieve not, rather find strength in what remains behind."

I had forgotten all that remained behind for me to enjoy, even though there had been significant loss. Grief, if used correctly, can be a gift that presents an opportunity to heal and grow; but I do suggest counseling. I couldn't have gotten the most from my precious life without it. Before I went to counseling, I felt sad and alone, and really couldn't move forward. It saved my sanity. I had to learn to find meaning in life again while treasuring the memories.

My mom gave me inspirational quotes almost daily, if not from the Bible, then from her favorite literature. I really loved this one: "Whatever you are facing today, keep going. Keep moving. Keep pressing on. There is a victory on the other side." And a powerful one from James Patterson: "Everything I loved was taken from me, yet I did not die."

I knew that God had not promised a life without pain, but He did promise that He would be there to give me strength to make it through the darkest days. I believed this without a shade of doubt. I knew that we can chose to learn and grow, or wilt and perish. I chose to grow. My mom said I was a strong woman and could make it through anything. "Just look at you now." There were days when I believed her, but mostly, I succumbed to the inner voices that came from Satan: You won't make it. You are not strong. Give up now. Why bother?

Everyone will offer suggestions on how to move forward, but again, there is no timeline. I've learned what not to say to people: "You are in a better place. It will all be okay someday. This must be the lesson that will catapult you to new happiness. It will be easier and all fade away someday." No, it won't! You must follow your own mind and heart, and you'll know when you are ready. I was grieving so many losses: my job, my career, my husband, my children, and my life. I had to learn that I needed to find something to do that would bring me happiness.

Teaching had provided that joy in the past. I filled my time by being around students, but now, that wasn't enough. I discovered pastimes I loved: writing, painting, jewelry, and crafts. Lastly, I learned that I would never forget what had happened and that was okay. Why would I want to forget? I had learned a lot from the experience, but now, I had to find the new me. I was like a phoenix rising from the ashes of my broken life. I had to embrace the new journey I was embarking upon. My favorite quote from Coralee was: "So far, you have survived 100 percent of your worst days. You are doing great." Coralee referred to a chart showing the points that you receive for specific incidents in your life. The more points you receive, the easier it is to have a mental breakdown. For instance, a death is worth ten points; a new job, eight points; relocation and a new home, eight points; etc. I had racked up enough points to have a mental breakdown, so I was grateful that I was in counseling with Coralee.

I thought about all the people I knew who needed counseling: Becky Sue's parents, Daniel Ray, Mr. Anderson, all the families of the students who had died—actually, everyone. I continued to meet with my counselor for six months, and then one day, she said, "You are graduating today. This is your last session. Call me if you need me."

I never called her again, but I think of her often. She, along with my mom, helped my soul survive. After each session, I would return to school and life renewed, refreshed, and alive. I could see progress—real progress. The nightmares stopped, and I slept well for the first time in years. I no longer needed medication to sleep. I could drown out the sad voices of the screaming children.

My mom said once you experience or see a tragedy, your mind and soul will never forget it or let it go. She was right. You just hide it or disguise it, but it is never really gone.

I started to compare myself to only myself, and I understood what Coralee had meant when she said, "Now go live, and practice the things I've taught you." And so I did. I was ever so grateful for the gift of forgiveness.

CHAPTER 28

Life After Easly

I DIDN'T THINK IT WAS POSSIBLE to be loved again, and to feel safe and okay with who I was. I was wrong...so wrong. Jonathan made me feel special. He erased the pain and shut the long chapter of suffering for good. He took an interest in me as a person. And I didn't just feel like a person again—I felt like an attractive, sexy older woman. It took years for me to share with Jonathan what had happened to me with Daniel Ray. He never asked questions. He figured when I was ready, I would tell him. He didn't know the public humiliation and private agony I had suffered. He cried with me as I poured out my soul and story, sparing no details.

He understood, being a retired police officer, a sergeant, and, later, a detective. He had worked on cases that dealt with false accusations, and saw the devastation and pain caused by the lies.

Jonathan was not shy about his opinions and willingly shared stories of his life and answered all my questions without hesitation. He had learned to stuff down his emotional pain, especially that involving his wife. He never gave up or complained. He was like a real-life Job in accepting his lot in life, believing that the Lord knew best and would direct him for good. He just didn't quit. He was so different from my first husband, whom I had both loved and feared. I didn't fear Jonathan; I only loved him. His enthusiasm and warm personality softened my fears, and his dynamic boldness made him unafraid to broach controversial subjects. That quality endeared him to me. After losing his wife and questioning his life, he learned to no longer fear anyone else's criticisms. He only feared the Lord.

We did share a love of the Lord, but our understanding was quite different. He had been raised with the Southern concept of a God who should be feared. I had been raised with the knowledge of the Lord's unconditional love for me, and therefore, I loved the Lord right back. We did share a passion for reading the Scriptures. On our darkest days, we both turned to the word of the Lord for solace. He would often leave notes with references to scriptures that brightened my day.

When we discussed what had happened to me, Jonathan said he would have leapt across the table in DCF court and strangled my lawyer and the investigator because of the way they were treating me. He said he would have protected me. He was sad that I had to go it alone, and he was incredulous that I had been scammed in that way. The principal should have been fired, and the kid should have been arrested. Jonathan said, "That's what happens to kids when their parents don't control them. They end up thinking they are so powerful that they can control other people's lives, and they damage themselves and the innocents in their path."

He had worked with troubled youth in a no-nonsense program. They would detain the offenders in jail overnight—partly to scare them, but mostly to educate them on prison life. He tried to persuade them to choose another path so that it was not their future. He was very successful, and many young people had thanked him for his caring and help. Prison life in the South was very different from other areas of the country. There were no "gym memberships," college programs, dinner choices, or craft classes to attend. There was hard labor, along with long work hours and lousy food. It was completely different from the prisons portrayed on television.

All along, I thought he didn't know about my past, but Jonathan said he heard people talk behind my back. Everyone had an opinion about me. He ignored the rumors and watched me conduct my life, and knew I was not only a good person, but that I was honest, and couldn't be the monster child abuser I was accused of being. I just couldn't be guilty of the things they talked about. He formed his own opinion of me, and it was a good one.

I was embarrassed when I found out that he knew everything. Mr. Detective had watched me, followed me once, and decided he liked me. He worked at the local Piggly Wiggly and always helped me with my groceries. He didn't need the money; he just needed to be with people. His grandchildren went to our school, and he would ask them about me. He received good reports, and decided to ask me out. It took me months, but I finally relented, and was so glad I did. He was the best. I thought, "Could I allow myself to be happy?"

At the same time, it was easy for me to trip into the bottomless pit of the past and fall into grieving mode again. The bad memories were sudden and sharp, and could overtake my mood and consume me. They needed to stay buried, but how was I to accomplish that when they could be unearthed so easily?

Jonathan started talking about marriage again, and I started to listen seriously this time. My mom wanted me to move back home. She had also lost track of my two sons. Fourteen years had passed, and they had to be pursuing their dreams—which didn't include me. She had sincerely tried to keep in touch with Philip, but he poisoned our sons' minds and badmouthed me, so they, too, lost interest in ever seeing me again.

This was damaging for my mom. She was their grandma, and she loved them deeply. They started to ignore her cards and letters and never returned her phone calls, and she knew it was over. My grandma used to say, "When I get old, please don't toss me aside in a corner like an old shoe." But that's exactly what they did. I wanted karma to take over. I wanted them to feel sorrow and be disgusted with their own behavior. They could treat me that way, but not their grandma.

My life demanded procedure and order rather than catering to personal feelings. I hadn't decided what to do. I could stay in Easly and marry Jonathan, or I could return to my home and live with and take care of my mom. She did need me. She was rapidly approaching ninety and wasn't as healthy as she had been. After all, she took care of me by constantly supporting me. She was always there for me. Do I stay at the school and continue to pretend I am a teacher? How long would that last? Do I try to make a go of it with Jonathan? Or do I go home? I had caused my mom to age rapidly, because she was always stressed out about me and my situation. I imagined she would have lived her life differently if I had been settled. I used to tell myself that I gave her a purpose in life. That was quite selfish, but it made me feel better—and less guilty.

For the present time, I decided to continue my pseudo-teaching job at school, and spend most of my free time with Jonathan. He was content with that for now. We planned to visit my mom at Thanksgiving. We were equally excited. My mom was elated that I would be visiting for almost a week, and I hoped it wouldn't cause me too much sadness to be home. My mom said, "You deserve to find someone and be happy." I thought that should happen after she died. I wanted her to meet and approve of Jonathan, but I feared she would think I was making another mistake by deciding to marry him. I hadn't had much luck picking out husbands. This trip would help me decide whether or not I should return to my home and live with Mom. I knew I was taking the chance of losing Jonathan, but I also knew I had to do what was morally right. I prayed for answer, and that whatever the answer turned out to be would sit well with Jonathan.

After living in Easly for so long, I felt comfortable and at home. I had fallen in love with Southern people, Southern food, and the Southern way of living. It wasn't perfect, but so much of it was right. I had never met such kind, helpful, caring people.

Take Otis Dawson, the owner of the only gas station in town. He was a poster child for helping. He was known to fix people's cars and not charge them if they couldn't afford it. I think he started the barter system in Easly. He would gladly have dinner in trade for changing someone's oil, and he considered that a fair trade.

Take Millie, one of the old-timers. We never knew her real age, but we guessed 108, according to Dr. McClain. One day, she needed to go to the hospital. Otis had found her nearly dead in her bedroom. He scooped her up in his arms, put her in the tow truck, and was about to take her to the hospital when she said, "I don't have my teeth." He quickly returned and looked for them. He found them in the commode, washed them off, and gave them to her. He never gave it a second thought. He always did the right thing. I had never forgotten that act of kindness. He taught me so much.

There were so many people, and so many examples of goodness. Miss Blanche Delilah Thompson, a second-grade teacher, had sheltered, fed, and cared for eleven foster children during her teaching career. Most of our students lived with a relative other than their parents. She ended up adopting two of those foster children. They still lived with her.

Then there was Atticus Fenton, who worked at the hardware store—a young, strong, kind gentleman. He was known to install car parts that were purchased at his store for free. One day, he was under a car repairing something, and felt a prick on his hand. He didn't think anything of it until he pulled his hand out and saw two small red holes indicating that he had been bitten by a snake. He drove himself to the hospital and was treated for a rattlesnake bite. It was actually the third time he had been bitten. The doctors said he must have built up an immunity, because he was released from the hospital just a few hours after receiving the antidote. The first time he was bitten, he spent three days in the hospital, and nearly died. I guess his body was used to it.

It was a common occurrence in Easly, snake bites—considering we had more snakes and bugs there than people. Once, while I was visiting an older woman in our local church community, I asked if I could help her with anything. She lived in a double-wide trailer at the far end of town. It was pretty roomy and attractive when you were inside the unit. You didn't even feel like you were in a mobile home. But on the outside, when you saw the skirting and the oil tank, it had no curb appeal.

Well, Miss Charlotte Cordelia asked me to do a load of wash for her, which I agreed to. She had a shed out back with a washer and dryer in it. You had to walk down a dirt path overgrown with high weeds and grass. I started to worry about snakes. Actually, I was petrified. I made it to the shed carrying the basket full of clothes without a snake encounter. Whew! I opened the shed door, turned on the light, and opened the lid to the washer. There, curled up inside the washer, was a rattler! I screamed, dropped the clothes, and ran back to Charlotte.

"I'm so sorry, Miss Charlotte, I can't do the wash. There's a snake in the washer."

She replied, "Just y'all git yourself a heapen' big stick and shew it away."

I said, "I just can't do that. I'll call someone else to help you."

I said my goodbyes, and ran to my car. I never went back there again. I will never get used to living with snakes. This would probably be the one reason I would ever leave Easly.

And, of course, Henrietta Calhoun had been the finest example of pure kindness. She did everything for everybody. I think she would have been like that even if she hadn't been rich. It was just her nature. She always kept food in her office: a big bowl of apples, and another bowl of pecans, sandwiches, and various items. It was always good, clean food; no junk. She said, "You cannot learn if you are hungry," and she noticed who was hungry. She would purposely invite children to her office to sample food. She would say, "I ain't sure which sandwich is the best. Could y'all please taste these, and let me know?" or "You know, I'm entering ma pecans in the fair. Try them, and y'all tell me if y'all think they the best y'all ever tasted."

Henrietta had been shrewd and creative. She made sure no one went hungry. She was known to send food home with many a child for their family. She started Backpack Fridays, only it was Brown Bag Fridays. She had boxes of food laid out in the all-purpose room for the children to choose from: fruit, nuts, muffins, beef jerky, and vegetables, of course; okra, boiled eggs, homemade bread, and sometimes treats from Honey Bee Bakery. They were most gracious, and not at all greedy. The rule was, you could take one of everything, but you had to promise to eat it all.

My least favorite thing about Easly was the snakes and bugs, but the food made up for it. I remember the first time I had chicken-fried steak—what an odd name for steak. It was outstanding. And now I couldn't imagine life without fried okra and baked beans. I was never a fan of pecan pie, but banana pudding pie was now a staple in my life.

I'm not saying there are not kind people where I came from; it's just that there seemed to be more of them in a small, poorer town. I had been welcomed without hesitation into the Easly family, and I had no regrets. I wasn't sure I wanted to leave Easly. I even had a Southern accent now, y'all. But the plans were set, and I would go visit home, accompanied by Jonathan.

My family welcomed Jonathan with open arms and open hearts. My two brothers loved him. They were fascinated that he carried two guns with him at all times—not just because he was a former police detective, but because of the fact that everyone carried guns in the South. It was accepted. They spent hours discussing life, both at home and in the South.

Jonathan made a great impression on my mom, showering her with gifts: teacups and teapots, lace doilies, a handmade scarf, and a South Carolina state flag. She approved of him, not because of his gifts, but because he was such a gentleman—a real Southern gentleman. I loved to hear him call me by name. "I just love your daughter Nail," he would tell my mom. We all laughed. He fit right in with the family. We spent two days visiting with family and friends, and two days touring the East Coast. He was impressed, but always compared everything to the South, naturally. I wasn't sure if he could ever live here, or if he even wanted to. He said he'd love to visit again. The key word there was visit.

After seeing my mom, I wasn't sure I could leave her. I wasn't sure I wanted to leave her or my home. It did feel good to be home, and see old friends and family. And you know what they say…there's no place like home. I thought maybe I should invest in a pair of ruby slippers, so I could visit whenever I wanted. Well, I didn't have to decide that day. I knew Jonathan wanted me to marry him and live with his family in South Carolina, but I also know that he would gladly visit my mom with me anytime. All I had to do was ask. What I didn't know was if he'd let me stay with my mom and visit him. Would he be patient and wait for me?

Our short visit ended with some smiles, but more tears. I promised my mom that I would be back soon, and I meant it. I just knew that I had to. My grandmother would say, "A mother can take care of ten children, but ten children cannot take care of one mother." She was right. Why was that true? I think Asian culture has successfully overcome that, but not American culture. We fill our lives with things and activities instead of memories of our family. Instead of spending time with our loved ones, we travel to spend time with strangers in strange places. Would we ever get it right? Would I make the right decision?

CHAPTER 29

The Awards Assembly

THE DAY FINALLY CAME. Mrs. Baxter said the mayor, the town council, the fire department, and the school board were all ready to meet and honor the heroes of the devastating fire, or the calamity, as we referred to it. I was not ready for this. I didn't think it was necessary for them to honor me, but I listened to Mrs. Baxter, who reminded me that Mrs. Calhoun and Becky Sue and her family would have wanted it this way. The arrangements included a tour of the new school and speeches from the principal, the fire chief, the mayor, and Mr. Sawyer, the father of Memphis, who had died in the fire.

Mrs. Penelope Baxter was schooled in the practices of serving as principal. More importantly, she had a heart big enough to love everyone with whom she came into contact. She had to fill Henrietta's shoes, and she was doing a great job. Many people compared her to Mrs. Calhoun, and she remained steadfast and held her ground when someone would say, "I don't think that is the way Henrietta would do that." She'd smile and say, "I did confer with her, and she is happy with my performance." That usually shut them up permanently. Mrs. Baxter had spent thirty-two years in the classroom, and she knew all the students very well. It wasn't a large enrollment, so she knew everyone by name. She was like Henrietta in a lot of ways: always willing to help anyone. She loved her family, and she loved the students.

Mrs. Baxter was an avid reader and was attempting to write a book herself. The faculty respected her, and she backed them and supported and fought for them… so unlike my former principal. She was doing an excellent job. She was fair, caring, knowledgeable, and visible. Just what you want in a principal. She held to her principles, and some parents thought she was too strict or harsh. She had a reputation to uphold, however, and she was accountable. Mrs. Baxter had to spend more time on the job, so her husband spent more time rearing their three children. He also learned a few more recipes, much to the kids' delight. It would all be worth the effort to sacrifice now, for her new job. She was the first of the four speakers.

Next, we heard from Wesley Griggs, the fire chief in Easly. Wesley came from a long line of firefighters. He was a little man in stature, but a giant in every other way. Wesley had been hurt in a fire eight years earlier, and was now confined to a wheelchair. He never let his disability stop him from bringing joy to others. He was as big as life. The kindergarteners liked to ride on his lap and wheel around the room. Wesley had several of his own grandchildren and a blended extended family with his new wife. His first wife hadn't been able to handle the outcome of the accident, so she divorced him. He spent two years recuperating, then he married his physical therapist, who was a widow and adored his spunk. It was easy to fall in love with Wesley. He was a competent fire chief, despite his injury.

We had our share of trials in Easly, but we also had our share of blessings too. Wesley always had a good attitude, even amidst the turmoil and sadness. He said we grow and learn from our experiences. I never saw him down or angry, except the day of the fire. We were all affected by it, but not as much as Wesley. As the fire chief, he felt an extra responsibility, as if he could have done more. He knew in his heart there was nothing else that could have been done, but he still felt guilty. I didn't think he would ever get over it. He was prepared to talk about forgiveness and joy. Joy in the morning, the morning of the resurrection. Wesley was quite a religious man. Had he not pursued this occupation, he might have been a preacher. He would have been a great one too. He had great faith, and wanted to wrap it around everyone like a warm blanket. To see his strength made you believe him and everything he said. He was a true hero...not me.

The mayor was slated to speak next. He was just an old Southern gentleman. Owen Jackson had been mayor as long as anyone could remember. No one had run against him, so he always won, even if that was against political rules. People thought, why change, if he is doing such a good job? I didn't know anyone who disagreed with him on politics. He listened to the people, and did what they wanted and needed. I don't even think he was associated with a party.

Mayor Jackson wasn't a Democrat or a Republican; he was a Southerner. He had a gun rack in his truck, and a smokehouse in his yard. He taught his boys how to hunt, camp, fish, and provide for their families. He'd teach those skills to anyone. He was a hard worker, and expected everyone to have the same work ethic he did. He was available to help you move in or out of town, and wasn't afraid to tell you which one you should do. He worked hard, and loved harder. He was in charge of everything, from the county fair to the barn dance to the potluck dinner to the local fundraiser. He would stand at the pulpit with all the authority he had and marry you or divorce you with love. And he did all these things well. Nobody messed with him. He had a kind heart, and would bail out a man who had drunk too much so he could go home and take care of his family. He saw the good in everyone, and that was why he was the mayor.

Violet Mobley, president of the board of education and town council, followed the mayor. She had three sisters named Rose, Magnolia, and Poppy. It was common for parents to name their girls after flowers. Her mom said she looked like a shrinking violet—hence the name. Well, Violet certainly proved her wrong; she was anything but shy. She held several positions in town, and held her head up high. She was independent, successful, sometimes controlling, and extremely focused on whatever project she was involved in at the moment. She taught her girls to be strong women. Besides her husband, there were no other men in the house. This fact allowed him the luxury of having his own bathroom, which he would occasionally share with the women.

Violet started out as the PTA president, but quickly climbed the ladder to president of the board of education and town council president. She said these positions went together neatly and complemented each other well. She had been a star cheerleader and drum majorette in high school and married shortly thereafter. She had three girls—boom, boom, boom—and never furthered her education. She wanted her girls to all graduate and marry later in life, and to have substantial careers. Though she loved her husband and girls, she secretly wished she had waited to marry and pursued a different path. Despite everything, she was content.

The last speaker was Cash Sawyer, father of Memphis Sawyer, who had perished in the fire. Cash was a humble man. He volunteered to speak because he loved his son so much, and he wanted everyone to know how much he and his wife and son had loved Mrs. Henrietta Calhoun. He began by praising the town and the people who had welcomed his little family when they moved to Easly. They never made them feel inadequate or poor, even though they barely had two pennies to rub together. Mrs. Calhoun always made sure Memphis had something to eat and extra milk, even though they couldn't afford to buy it. The teachers made a special effort to love Memphis. He struggled in school, but never felt badly about it. No one made fun of him. Each day, he would come home with wondrous tales to tell about Henrietta, his teachers, his classmates, and everything he had learned. He was such a happy child.

"Thanks to all of you. You made my son happy during his short life. I am so grateful that we chose to move to Easly and be part of this great family. I am so grateful for this school and the heroes who saved your children. It was the hardest thing we had ever done to bury our son, but it was the sweetest feeling to know he was in the arms of Mrs. Calhoun. I am glad we voted to refurbish the school and keep the memories safe here. Thank you all for that you have done."

Mr. Sawyer received the loudest applause. Everyone agreed with his sentiment. They were happy that we had our school, our teachers, and our town.

Plaques and awards were passed out, and refreshments were served. The entire town was invited. Mrs. Baxter had extended the invitation to all the families of the deceased children in addition to the Calhoun and Blackmoore families.

All of Mrs. Calhoun's family replied that they would attend, which included seven children and many grandchildren and great-grandchildren. They would be coming from California, Colorado, Illinois, Maine, and right here in South Carolina.

Mr. Blackmoore had passed away a year after his wife died, I think of a broken heart. Their three children still lived in Easly, and would attend with their children.

Of the families that had moved away, only three would return to attend the assembly: Becky Sue Belmont's family, Kent Austin's family, and Billy Deluke's family.

Locally, the Sawyers, the Jeffersons, the Masons, and the Boone families would attend.

The parents and families of the four students I had saved all responded yes to their invitations. They included Buddy Ray Preston's family, Dixie Taylor's family, Georgia Lawson's family, and Charles Jackson's family. It would be a difficult time for everyone, even though almost two years had passed. Certain memories always seem fresh.

Buddy Ray Preston lived with Alma, his great-grandma. She called her grandson, Daniel Ray, the father of Buddy Ray, in New York to invite him to the ceremony. Apparently, he and his girlfriend had had the baby boy, but neither of them felt they could raise him, so they packed him up and sent him to Easly to be raised by his great-grandma and great-grandpa, who gladly agreed. Buddy's dad promised to visit often, contribute financially to his upbringing, and keep in touch. None of these things actually happened. Buddy's dad was always in trouble with the law and life in general, and knew he couldn't take care of himself, let alone a baby. He'd had a rough time in school, and nearly didn't graduate. His mom was a mess, and hadn't shown much caring or any parental skills. She herself had had her first of six kids at age sixteen. I guess it was expected that Buddy's dad was destined to fail.

His grandma decided that wasn't going to happen to her great-grandson Buddy. She loved him, and then she loved him some more. Buddy's dad visited frequently in the beginning, but as the years passed, he became preoccupied with his own life and sent an occasional birthday gift or card, then lost touch completely. It reminded me of my sons. At first, they had kept in touch with my mom; but then, shortly thereafter, she became a memory too—just like me.

After the fire and almost losing his only child, Buddy Ray's dad felt his heart soften, and he decided maybe he should raise his son. His grandma questioned him about it daily. "How are you going to do it? Where will you get the money to pay for everything? Who will watch him when you go to work? He is settled here. He is happy here. I can take care of him better than you can. I think it's best that the boy stay with me."

Buddy Ray's great-grandma reminded me of my mom. She was a strong woman who had lived through many trials but kept her wits about her, her faith in God, and her ability to love. She was so similar to my mom, the matriarch. Everyone looked up to my mom. Buddy Ray's great-grandma would say, "You don't live to be eighty-five and not know things. Your years teach you so much. You learn to choose your battles—the ones you can win. You learn the right way to do things. Even though your children and grandchildren don't believe you, you know in your heart you are right. Your years of experience have corroborated that to you." Most importantly, she was raising Buddy Ray with this attitude about life. Love everyone, forgive everyone, and you will be happy.

His dad insisted that he try it his way, and took Buddy Ray to New York. He actually lasted three weeks before he called and said he would be bringing Buddy back to South Carolina. He came to his senses. His grandma didn't reprimand him. Instead, she said she understood, and she just loved them both. "I knew it was best for him to stay with me, and you are welcome to stay also. I love you—I have and always will love you, and don't you ever forget that. You should visit more." Buddy Ray's dad promised that he would make a bigger effort to visit his son, and even send money occasionally to help his grandma. Well, that didn't happen, but now that he had been invited to the assembly, his heart softened again, and he decided to attend and even stay a little longer—and maybe reconnect with his son.

Buddy Ray's dad remembered the summer months he had spent with his grandparents in South Carolina. It was always an adventure, with creeks to swim in, fish to catch, trees to climb, caves to explore, and kids to play with. He was never in trouble in Easly. He had too much to do, and school was not a part of it. He helped on the farm and respected his grandparents. In fact, he respected anyone older than himself. His grandma held him to different standards. He had chores to do, and was expected to be responsible and accountable. He cultivated good habits with the help of his grandparents. There just weren't enough hours of daylight to do all that he wanted to do, and never enough to do all he had to do.

My mom was raised on a farm, and she said farm kids aren't troublemakers. I believed it. You don't have time to get in trouble. You also see and learn about life differently. She said after you watched animals being born—cows, chickens, horses—you looked at life differently. You respected the whole process to a greater extent. And you seemed to understand life more.

Dan had a different set of friends in Easly, kids who

were mostly poor financially but rich in every other area. They were rich in family, memories, customs, and, most importantly, love. They seemed well-balanced, stable, and content. After a while, he was, too. They were God-fearing people, and attended church regularly and willingly. It was part of their culture. He went to church regularly for the first time in his life, and enjoyed it. His grandparents were there, and so were his friends. It seemed like more than religion. It was customary, like being with family. He could see why the church was packed every Sunday. It fulfilled a purpose for many. The weekly sermon provided answers to many questions, and the preacher appeared to be sincere, calling you by name as he shook your hand before leaving church. He always had some kind words to say to Dan, which made him like him even more.

Why was it different when he went home? What went wrong whenever he returned to his hometown? Every August, he cried when he had to leave and return to the crowded, noisy city. He promised he'd write to his grandparents, and couldn't wait to see them again. That was why he decided to send his son to be raised with his grandparents. He knew it was the right decision for Buddy Ray to be with them. He wanted his son to have a better chance than he'd had at life. He knew he would be fine—no, better than fine, he would be outstanding, and have all the love he needed. Dan missed the country life. He missed the peace of it, but mostly, he missed the love he had felt in Easly. At least his mom had the sense to do that right. She should have left him there permanently. His life would have been better all around. He wouldn't have been so discontented or feel like such a failure if he had stayed in Easly. Oh, how he wished he had stayed.

So now he was coming back to his favorite town, to his favorite people, to participate in one of the most important days of his life. He thanked God that his son had been spared, and committed to trying harder to be a better father, to be honest and true, and to set a good example for him. He even toyed with the idea that he could meet some nice Southern belle and marry, and settle down and have more children.

His grandma said it was never too late to begin again. She said she would keep her eyes open for someone who would be just perfect for him. And she did. She knew a girl around his age who worked at Honey Bee Bakery, and was so sweet. She was hoping she could fix them up soon. He had to promise to stay and get to know her and change. He had to be the kind of man who would deserve that kind of girl. His grandma said, "Always be the kind of person you would want to marry."

Dan came a week before the awards assembly and stayed at the old familiar farm. There weren't any animals there now except for some barn cats. He wandered into the barn, remembering all the good times he'd had there during his childhood. He decided that tomorrow, he would take his son fishing after school at the creek where he used to fish. He would pack a lunch and spend quality time with Buddy, just the two of them. He could try to make up for lost time. After school, he was waiting with the rods and lunch and a heavy heart. "Hey Buddy, ready to show your pa how to fish?" Buddy nodded his head as he grabbed his dad's hand and started to skip along the dirt road. His dad wiped a tear from his eye, thinking about how much he had missed. But Grandma had said he could start today.

"So, how do like living here in Easly?"

"I just loves it here, Dad. Are y'all gonna stay here with us? Y'all can sleep in my bed. I can sleep on da floor. I's hopin y'all can stay."

"I don't know how long I can stay. We'll see. I have to work out some things first."

"Okay Dad, race ya to da creek!"

Dan loved this interaction. Why had he ever left Buddy here? Why hadn't he stayed with him? He would have to work some things out, but he was leaning toward the thought of staying. They sat on the ground near the edge of the water. It was a perfect day. They sat in silence until Buddy Ray caught something on his line. He showed his dad how to reel it in just the way his great-granddad had showed him.

"See, Dad, this is how y'all do it. Y'all wanna try?"

"Yes, son, I do. Thanks for teaching me."

The day continued in pure joy for both of them. Buddy Ray didn't show any animosity toward his dad. He just accepted the fact that his great-grandma had said he was away, and couldn't come see him right now.

Buddy Ray had been so excited when his great-grandma told him his dad was coming. He told everyone at school.

He said, "Miss Billie, guess what? My dad is coming to the awards assembly all the way from that big city. Wait till y'all meet him. You gonna like him."

"I'm sure I will, Buddy Ray. I'm looking forward to it."

They were inseparable that week, playing and talking before and after school. Dan wanted to talk to Buddy Ray about the fire and thank the teacher who had saved him. He thought maybe it would be difficult, so he decided to wait until the assembly, where he could meet her in person and thank her for saving his son's life. It would be tomorrow soon enough.

The principal, the fire chief, the mayor, and some of the teachers greeted everyone as they filed into the Augusta Blackmoore Media Center. No one was surprised by the great turnout. There were no empty seats. Some people were standing in the back. The families of the deceased were in the first two rows of chairs. Behind them sat the faculty and their families. On stage sat Mrs. Baxter, the fire chief, the mayor, the president of the town council, and Mr. Sawyer. The awards recipients were seated throughout the auditorium. I was sitting near the back with Jonathan. Anyone who wanted to was invited to tour the school, then make their way back to the auditorium for the presentation.

During the next forty-five minutes, we listened to all of these speakers praise our principal and kindergarten teacher and talk about each of the twelve lost students individually, citing their accomplishments. Then they called the "heroes" onto the stage: eight volunteer firefighters and myself. I didn't want to go up, but Jonathan pushed me out of my seat. We stood onstage as the crowd gave us a standing ovation accompanied by thunderous applause. I felt embarrassed. I watched as Mrs. Baxter presented a plaque to each person inscribed with their name and words of gratitude.

As they called my name and I approached Mrs. Baxter, Buddy Ray Preston jumped up from the front row and yelled "Yeah, Miss Billie!" We'd had a special bond since I saved him from the fire. I turned to look at him, and saw his dad pulling him down. I looked at his dad, and knew his face. I knew that face.

It was the face of Daniel Ray Sawyer. The Daniel Ray. The boy who had caused me to lose my job, my career, my life! He was the father of Buddy Ray Preston. How could it be? How did I not know? His middle name was Ray, but they had different last names. I had never connected the dots. Buddy Ray's dad was from New York, and his grandparents were raising Buddy Ray. Daniel Ray had once destroyed my life, and now I had saved that of his son. How ironic. Buddy Ray's great-grandma had never spoken his name. Buddy had said, "I can't wait for you to meet him...my dad. Y'all gonna love him, Miss Billie."

Our eyes locked, and Daniel Ray started to cry. He knew the truth, and now he had to face it. His son had said, "You'll meet her, the teacher who saved me." He never said my name until he yelled out, "Miss Billie."

I stared at Daniel. I had such mixed feelings for him. I wanted to hate him, to scream at him, to ruin his life like he'd ruined mine. But that was so long ago, and I'd learned to forgive everyone. Then my heart softened, and as I stared at Daniel Ray, I mouthed the words, "I forgive you." He nodded his head and acknowledged my words. Now I knew what it meant to feel peace and power, just as Coralee had taught me. The gift of forgiveness was complete. It was over. It was done.

EPILOGUE

Going Back Home

I MADE MY DECISION TO GO HOME. Many factors influenced my decision. Daniel Ray would now live in Easly. Even though I had forgiven him, it was still difficult to see him. My mom was getting on. She was nearly ninety years old, and she really needed me. Jonathan said he still wanted to see me. He suggested that we visit each other. I didn't believe it would work—long-distance romances usually die—but I smiled and said, "I'd like that."

He said he wasn't ready to give up on me yet. "Is there anything I can say to persuade you to stay?"

I cried, and we hugged for a long, long time. "No, there isn't, but I hope you meant it when you said we could see each other."

I meant it, but I guess Jonathan hadn't. We saw each other a couple of times. We visited both at home and in South Carolina, but it didn't last. I knew it wouldn't.

How could it? I don't blame him. It was not reasonable. I had to take care of my mom; she needed me. I knew I had sacrificed my future, yet it didn't seem like a sacrifice. I know the Lord wouldn't punish me for doing what was right. There would be blessings to come, after all. I thought about my life in Easly. It was so long ago, yet still fresh in my thoughts. I had grown and changed so much since those days. I was older now, but so much wiser. I knew what my mom meant when she said, "Your years bring you great knowledge." I reviewed everything in my mind like a video on fast-forward. So much had happened: good and bad. I had made lasting friendships. Maybe I would return to Easly someday. I knew I would be welcome.

I haven't heard from Jonathan again. I didn't expect to, but I secretly hoped he would call me. I miss him. Oh, well, I guess it is over. Onward and upward to newer and better things.

Being home is not as strange as I thought it would be. I had to find a job. Having my wonderful, strong, brilliant mom still around helps every day. None of my friends have living moms. I am lucky. Her keen mind and positive attitude add to the pleasure of caring for her. She really does take care of me, though.

I met with my old friends and teachers with whom I taught years earlier. We gathered for lunch, and they would inevitably discuss school, lessons, principals, and students. It was so painful for a long time. Just the thought of discussing these subjects made me cringe.

Sometimes, I would excuse myself and leave early. At other times, I would sit through the conversation, trying to change the emphasis from school to anything else. I knew they meant well, but it was still uncomfortable for me, and soon after that, I stopped meeting with them. I shared my concerns, and noticed that they asked me less and less to join them, except for my best friend Lee. She always stood by me. She had always believed I was innocent. She'd fight to the death for me. I still see her all the time.

I am a realtor now, and have been for years, since I moved back home. Interestingly enough, I have seen many of my old students in a variety of places since moving back home. Many of them have stayed in their hometown. I met a student pumping gas who recognized me, and asked how I was doing and if I was still teaching. I met another one in the grocery store, and he introduced me to his wife and children. He said he had such fond memories of my science class. Another was working as a bank teller. She told me she loved the experiments we did in class on Fridays. And one of my favorite students, who was now a salesgirl, said she still had the solar system project she had made in my eighth-grade science class.

Recently, a former student called me to help her buy a house. That was a fun experience. Again, I was teaching in a different venue. We found exactly what she wanted, and she was ecstatic. She thanked me over and over. Another student, who considered me a mom, invited me to go with her to her timeshare in Mexico, which I did, and had a fantastic time. One more who moved cross-country invites me to all the major events in her life. I have attended her college graduation, her wedding, and the baptism of her first child. And last month, when my car died, the tow-truck driver said, "Aren't you Mrs. Murray, my science teacher? I'd know you anywhere. You look great, you haven't changed. I loved your class."

I also accepted a position as a Sunday school teacher in my church, which helps fill the void of not teaching. It's not enough. I miss teaching and am still sad about it, especially at this stage of my life. I should be retiring with teacher's benefits, but I'm not.

I have made a positive impact on many students and changed many lives. I am thankful for that. I am also thankful for this career opportunity, which allows me to make my own schedule and do what I want or need to do. I have been able to help take care of three aunts and uncles, including moving them, cleaning their homes, planning their funerals, and burying them. I would never have been able to do any of this as a teacher. I've also been able to take care of my ninety-year-old mom and keep her in her own home. My change in occupation allowed me to do this. It is true what they say: when a door closes, a window opens. I have been spared many a hardship. I've been able to support myself in my new career. I still find myself questioning how different things could have been had I never met Daniel Ray. I guess I'll never know.

ABOUT THE AUTHOR

Neile Parisi is the author of *Today My Name Is Billie* based upon an incident in her life as an eighth grade teacher. Neile taught school for eighteen glorious years in public schools. She experienced both joy and tragedy in her classroom, but continually loved her students. Following her teaching career she became a Registered Sanitarian. Having a Masters Degree in Health Education, she was able to use her teaching skills to help educate workers in the restaurant world, teaching proper food handling skills, provide knowledge about radon, asbestos, and lead poisoning to home owners, investigate food poisoning, test beach water and pools for bacteria levels, inspect restaurants, day cares, schools and hospitals, and at times even trapping rats and rodents. Currently she is a realtor, who by the way, won Second Place in The Woman's Arm Wrestling competition in Las Vegas, and promises she won't let anyone "Twist Your Arm." She is also a stand-up comic on the weekends, drawing from her varied background of occupations. This is her first novel.